Wets seb cuah?

"GOOD LUCK, CHARLES," JULIE chimed in. She lit two cigarettes and offered me one. I shook my head and Steve grabbed it from her, taking a huge drag and inhaling deeply.

"He doesn't need any luck, Julius Caesar!" Steve asserted. I noted that the T-shirt he wore under his denim jacket bore the words "FUCK THE XP" beneath an image of a frowning dwarf holding a battleaxe.

Mike had retreated a few paces to a small stone altar set up several feet from the well opening. "Leave him," he said as he lit two black candles.

Julie and Steve maneuvered themselves beside Mike.

"*Zod manas zi ba!*" Mike intoned, eyes closed, hands held out toward the sky. "*Zazas! Zazas! Nasatanada zazas!*" He opened his eyes and gazed at me. I could almost believe that they had become pits of black fire blazing in the midst of his angular, vampiric face.

I saluted once and sidled off the edge, into the darkness below...

FEAR CLUB
A CONFESSION

FEAR CLUB
A CONFESSION

THE MEANS OF ESCAPE

BOOK ONE

DAMIAN STEPHENS

FOURTH MANSIONS PRESS
CHARLOTTESVILLE, VIRGINIA

FEAR CLUB: A Confession
The Means of Escape
Book One

FOURTH MANSIONS PRESS, LLC
Charlottesville, Virginia

fourthmansions.com

ISBN: 978-0-578-46466-4

Cover art by Pantelis Politakos
Cover design by Fourth Mansions Press, LLC

Box 1132
(I'm pretty sure it will work.)

CONTENTS

prologue

REMEMBER

R EMEMBER! THE MANY WORLDS and the means of escape!

I'm taking pen to paper and recording it all. You know, *the* pen. (That ought to get it over to you without too much in the way of incomprehensibility.) I hope it makes a difference; I hope that you will find this and I hope that you will remember. The parts that I wasn't there to witness I pieced together as best I could from what I was told. The rest of it—as for the rest of it, well, I tried to write it the way it happened.

If I got some of it wrong, then *remember it for me*—write it down, try to figure out a way to get it to me. And if anything *else* goes wrong, I hope that you still have the lighter—just burn it. There may be good reason to.

Don't worry about us. For the moment, we're in the Emporium. It turns out there's a post office here, too—of course. (I think I mention it later.) Roland tells me that on your side, where we're guessing you are right now, there's a post office

3

across the street, and someone who will be able to retrieve this and leave it where you can find it. We put something of a reminder for whoever *does* retrieve this on the dedication page, just to be sure. (Creepy, right?)

Roland also tells me, perhaps unfortunately, that there may be—probably *will* be—at least one transmission error, for which I apologize right off the bat.

But please remember! We want you to know, at least, if nothing else: we miss you. (I steadfastly refuse to pass along what your dear old pal just told me to say.)

part one

FEAR CLUB

I FELT MORE ANXIOUS on the way home.

"Mike's got it in for me," I told Julie. I typically walked with her back down to South Street, at the very edge of town where she lived, then cut through the forest on Chicken Hill to get back to my own house. Steve had cut and run—his evasive remarks made it obvious he was going to score drugs of one form or another.

Julie gave her usual derisive snort. "Mike's got it in for everyone," she said. "Death just doesn't seem afraid of him yet. He'll keep trying. Meanwhile, he's going to experiment on us."

"How am I supposed to take that?"

"When we lower you into that old well, put a smile on your face and give him a thumb's up." Julie looked suddenly pensive. "Come to think of it, that might kill him."

I laughed. "Be sure to let everyone know it was my fault."

Julie pulled a warped cigarette out from a package in her jeans pocket and lit it. We walked in silence for a few moments. Although Steve and Julie had been friends (off and on) since kindergarten, and both had known me only since the Bhairavi Society had been inaugurated by Michael Flowers, I felt somehow perfectly safe when confiding in Julie. I still wasn't too sure about Steve, admittedly, nor his motives in any respect.

"What if it's true?" I had to bring it up. We had all "kind of" talked about it at intervals, but never seemed to come to anything more than speculative conclusions.

Julie took a long drag off of her cigarette and

exhaled. Nicotine-laden contrails scurried through her blue-black hair. "If it's true then we're done. We win. Mike goes to heaven, or whatever."

"And Curwen Flowers? It would all be true." I waved my hand at the streetlamps which burned a soft orange against the night sky. "None of this would be necessary anymore. 'No more school, no more books,' and all that."

Julie's home appeared ahead, off to the right, at the foot of Chicken Hill. We paused so that she could finish her cigarette.

"Forgive me if I don't get too excited about it," she said. "We're probably fools to listen to him. No—we're *definitely* fools for listening to him. But the fact remains—"

"He really does know something," I finished for her. We had all seen it: myself, Julie, Steve. That incredible night two years ago, and we were the *only* ones to have seen it, and there was nothing we could say to anyone about it. There was nothing we could do except agree to Mike's wild plans, believe his wild tales, and put our faith in the wild magic he had demonstrated that night.

For all intents and purposes, to the rest of the world, Mike Flowers would have to stay dead—at least, until we had discovered the means of escape for ourselves. Dragged into his dream, we could only live out the story and hope that its author's madness proved somehow more durable than the cold, sane world none of us could ever return to.

I MADE IT THROUGH the woods that night by instinct, as usual, but not without a certain added concern for dark shapes rustling in the trees and bushes, barely containing their glee at my imminent demise.

Once back home, I climbed the trellis to my bedroom window. The moon, I noticed, peeked out from behind clouds scudding past. It seemed peculiarly intent on me, on the goings-on in and around Golem Creek. *Is this the sensation that death provides?* I wrote in my journal. *Everything begins to glow with a strange light, like in a dream, where everything lives because it's all part of you.*

And perhaps its awareness is your own awareness, and its fear your own as well.

How sleep came I don't remember. A blackout. Before I knew it, I was up and on my way to school, having barely seen my parents at all. This wasn't unusual, but it was something I was suddenly very conscious of.

Molly Furnival. English composition. The gods shone down as best they could upon her, perhaps aware of their own inability to properly shadow forth such perfection, such inexhaustible beauty, such—

"—idiocy? Charles, please wake up."

Mrs. Hurtangle rapped gently on the podium before her. Molly gazed at me, as did Steve (clearly about to burst with laughter) and the rest of the class. How some of us had gotten *into* AP English was beyond me.

"The text? Charles? What does it have to do with idiocy?" She waved a copy of Dostoevsky's *The Idiot* before the class.

This would require cleverness.

"I'm pretty sure—I mean—" I began.

"Nothing," Molly said. "I mean, not in the usual sense. It's a translation, first of all, of course."

Mrs. Hurtangle smiled. "Go on."

"But being an idiot means living in your own world, not seeing the world that everyone else lives in."

Mrs. Hurtangle was obviously pleased. "There! Yes. Very good. The word derives from the Greek *idios*, which basically means 'private.' The rest of the world, the common world, is *koinos*, or shared. It's just this common world that an 'idiot' either does not see, does not experience, or *rejects*."

I tried to formulate a grin which, I hoped, did not make me look like an idiot in the usual sense. Molly would have to wait until the next life, I supposed, the one where I had any chance of going to Yale or Harvard or some place like that. The one where I might actually have something to offer her besides admiration.

"In a sense, then," Mrs. Hurtangle continued, "being an idiot is a necessary precursor to changing the world outside of you. Being so stubbornly preoccupied with your own internal world that the world around you either *adapts* to you or *destroys* you. You may have heard the old observation: 'The truth is first laughed at, then viciously fought against, and finally accepted as self-evident.' The idiot is one who upholds what he or she considers 'true' until the world changes."

"Or until they die," I said.

Mrs. Hurtangle grinned. "Certainly, Charles. Glad to know that you're paying attention. Now are there any—"

"Why don't people see what's true right off the bat?" I asked.

Molly chanced a look over at me, then jotted something down in her notebook.

"How do you mean, Charles?" Mrs. Hurtangle asked.

"Well," I said, "if we live in a real world with real things, and what's true corresponds with what's real, then how can anyone ever miss that? How can we *start out* not knowing what's real? Doesn't that seem weird to anyone?"

There were a few murmurs of what I took to be appreciation from the rest of the class. Then the inevitable.

"That's what learning is." This from Pete Jarry, one of the "back of the class" kids. Steve bought grass from him occasionally, so we knew he was at least okay. I recalled Mike saying something about Pete's brother Stek at one point, something about part of the prophecy. And everyone had heard all about the weird things Stek had been claiming he saw.

"Your brain starts out dumb," Pete continued. "Its job is to map out the world around it, but sometimes it gets things wrong, like when you try to draw something and, even though you *know* exactly what it looks like, you can't seem to draw it right. So you learn more and your map gets better."

"Thank you, Pete," Mrs. Hurtangle said. Pete waved and grinned. Seeming remarkably sober today, he resumed leaning back in his chair and gazing up at the ceiling. I happened to notice Molly looking at him with a mixture of—what was it? Caution—and perhaps interest? Did *my* Molly (not to put too proprietary a turn on it) have a *thing* for—gods be damned—*Pete*?

"That's a particularly sound response," Mrs. Hurtangle continued. "There was an entire field of study based around this idea called 'cybernetics,' developed in the mid-twentieth century, when people were trying to understand how to optimize learning strategies, both in humans and, potentially, in machines. Another famous quote also ties into this: 'The map is not the territory.'"

The bell rang, evoking its usual chaos.

"It looks like we'll have to continue our discussion next time. Thank you all for some great comments today! Be sure to continue with the reading—"

I was already out the door. I usually tried to get the hell out of English as quickly as possible, so that I wouldn't have to feign brilliance around Molly.

"Charles?"

It was Molly. How did she get out here so fast?

"Uh." Perfect start, Charley, as always.

"I liked your comment." She stood there before me, those strange lavender eyes of hers wide and somehow glittering in the fluorescent light. "I've thought about that before. No one's ever put it quite so bluntly, though."

"Yeah. Well." Was I staring? I think I was staring. Should I say something? "That's me, you know. Blunt."

Beautiful.

Thankfully, Molly laughed. Was she blessed in all possible respects? Even her teeth were flawless. "Okay," she said. "Anyway. I just wanted to say. You know."

She began to walk off.

"What are you doing on Halloween?"

Oh, gods, no. That was me. *I* said that. *But I'm supposed to DIE on Halloween night...*

Molly paused and turned back around to face me. "I don't know for sure. I think I'll be at Amanda Whitfield's party for a little while, at least. Are you going?"

"Hey, Charley." It was Pete Jarry. What the hell did he want? "You got a minute?" He seemed to be waving a sheet of paper at me. From this distance, it looked like a grid of random letters.

Recover—*please!* "Sure am," I blurted out to Molly. *What?!?*

Pete was being overrun by the chaos in the hallway. I waved at him, and continued failing myself with the love of my life.

"Great! I guess I'll see you there?" she said.

I resigned myself to it. "Yes. Definitely."

She turned and walked off, still smiling. A crowd of impudent mortals, fathomless, flowed past me in the corridor; I, mere scurf amongst them, stood, astonished by my self-betrayal. Was that a date I had just made? Or at least an outline of one?

Pete had disappeared in the chaos. Whatever it was must not have been overly important. I'd have to ask Steve later if he knew what it was about.

Only one thing kept me from utter despair:

if I *did* survive the Ordeal on Saturday, I might have the courage to ask Molly out on a real date at the party afterward. Mike wasn't going to be pleased, though. The Ordeal was to be followed by an all-night vigil to ensure that The Ones Beyond were fully propitiated. What if the Descent actually revealed what Mike had implied it was going to? A solution, however nebulous, to all of our mundane problems?

I supposed that—despite my situation with Molly *technically* falling into the category of "mundane problems"—after I died, Mike was probably going to kill me for this.

I HAD DONE THIS type of thing before.

Darkness, I remember vividly. Thick, deep *darkness*; even more frightening for the fact that I did *not* feel as if I would suffocate in it—I felt as if I could reach out or fall forever, and never touch a thing...

It was the crawl space beneath the house on Brake Street first, the house behind which was the grotto of ash trees within which Mike's hovel sat, where all the meetings of the Bhairavi Society—or "Fear Club," as Steve called it—took place. I felt relatively certain, as I slid on my belly through dank, decrepit, mold-ridden passageways, provided with no light or protection of any sort, that the "heart's blood" ingredient of the "elixir" Mike had all of us partake of prior to this was something like LSD or finely powdered *Stropharia cubensis*. The earth beneath me began to come alive; everything wriggled, everything lived. How many black widows were down here? How many scorpions? How many rats driven mad by hydrophobia?

But that was the point of the Bhairavi Society: "live as one dead, and death cannot truly take you." We believed because we had seen it with our own eyes. And Mike swore that he knew the Way, and that it would be revealed to us as well if we implicitly trusted him.

Steve had been buried alive. Mike had somehow secured an oxygen tank which *supposedly* provided several hours' worth of air. He had encased the air meter in black electrical tape so that no one could see if the (admittedly somewhat rusty-looking) tank actually held anything. Steve dug his own grave one night in Chesterfield Woods just outside of town, lay down in it, and allowed us to fill it back in over him. Patting down the dark, musty soil with one of the shovels, knowing that Steve was down there, was bad enough; Mike insisted on placing a stone at the head of the gravesite and performing a brief ritual service that would "entomb his fear," as he put it.

We waited, mostly in silence—too long, as far as I could tell. After a while, we began to think that Mike had no intention of rescuing Steve. "His fate is sealed," was all Mike said when I inquired regarding when we should start exhuming him.

Julie, as usual, didn't seem nervous at all. What did she know that I didn't know?

As my anxiety reached a pitch, we began to notice the earth over Steve's body shifting and moving. Mike became noticeably energized, and before long a muddy hand broke through the soil's surface.

"He has been tested! He has passed the Ordeal!" Mike's elation was shared by the rest of us—although, I suspected, not for the same reasons. If I recall correctly—the memory is somewhat obscured by my relief at not being accomplice to murder—Steve had smiled in a dazed way, shaking out filthy hair and clothes, and said: "Sure beats dinner and a movie."

I was not certain what Julie's Ordeal involved. Somehow, she "passed through" without an audience. Mike casually mentioned her successful "testing" weeks later during an otherwise typical meeting without giving any explicit details. Steve and I both knew not to ask questions of Mike, who would only make some obscure or clichéd comment about things anyway.

But I kept waiting for the right moment to ask Julie herself.

"It was...really fucked up," was all she told me, one night after the monthly meeting. "I'm not supposed to say anything more about it."

"Or what?" I asked.

"Or one of us *really* dies."

Given the circumstances, I didn't press the issue or try to call anyone's bluff. Mike might seem like a lot of talk at times, but when dealing with an undead lunatic, your first assumption should probably be that they've got nothing to lose by following through on threats.

FRIDAY NIGHT, THE EVE of All Hallows' Eve, I took a walk, alone, through my neighborhood. Jack-o'-lanterns glared menacingly from porches. Fake cobwebs hung abundantly in trees above lawns decked out like graveyards with tombstones sporting clever epitaphs.

In my search/ For miraculous powers/ I trusted my life/ To Mike-Goddamned-Flowers!

Etc.

A cool autumn breeze blew skittering leaves across the sidewalks, and I breathed deep. I didn't *really* think I was going to die. I felt strangely honored that I had been chosen to "descend," as Mike had put it—something about my survival at the Brake Street house must have impressed him, although I felt that being buried alive had to have been worse.

Near the back of the neighborhood, I noticed a faint light playing about in the woods near the top of Chicken Hill. Flashlight? But that was near the Murk—who would be up there tonight...?

Mike. Preparing for tomorrow night? *Was he planting something for me to find tomorrow? Was the Ordeal a blind, a fake, a magic trick? Were* all *of the Ordeals fakes?*

I glanced about me, then chose a path between two houses and started up the hill. The going was not particularly easy, not by way of the route I planned on taking, but I felt confident that if I could stick to one of the thin, older paths that wound around the southern side of the hill, I might be able to catch a glance of whoever was up there.

Luckily, the moon shone down clearly on the hillside. That did not, however, imply that I was able to pick my way across rubble and fallen branches with the utmost accuracy. All I could hope for was that "whoever it was" would still be up there by the time I arrived, and try to keep as silent as possible just before cresting the hill.

I did trip—once—but other than that I was able to keep pretty quiet. Having scaled this hill countless times, the going wasn't all that bad. It was what I saw when I peeked over a fallen log and gazed into the darkness by the Murk that almost caused me to cry out and lose my advantage.

It was Mike, all right, but the *thing* with him appeared not only inhuman, but as close to a devil or demon as anything I'd ever imagined or seen in the movies.

"...as soon as you can. They have received the location and await the items." Mike spoke to the thing, which towered over him by several feet, hunched back and mottled, reptilian skin glinting by the dim glow of Mike's flashlight. Its head, which bore large black pits for eyes and something resembling a mouth, seemed too large for its thin, serpent-like neck, which curved like a vulture's over a strangely flabby torso. Clawlike hands dwarfed thin arms which quivered occasionally, hanging evilly from sharply pointed shoulders.

The thing appeared to respond, but with no voice like any I'd ever heard. I could not make out anything of what it said—a dark, deep rumbling coupled with thunking clicks and moans were all it resembled.

"I have plans for her," Mike said when the thing had paused. It lifted its head and opened wide its eyes, a rapid, low-pitched clicking emerging from its half-open mouth.

"As I said, I have plans for her. You can thank Laban for it, if we ever see him again." The thing began nodding its head rapidly and lightly stomping its shaggy, goat-like legs. "Go, now. And give uncle my regards."

The thing raised its head briefly as if in salute, then turned and skulked to the edge of the Murk. In the darkness, it appeared as if it melted into shadow and somehow funneled into the well.

Mike turned rapidly in my direction. I ducked behind the log, but heard nothing—no confrontation, no challenge. Slowly I raised my head and peeked over the log again.

Michael Flowers was gone without a trace.

SATURDAY MORNING. HALLOWEEN.

I awoke before sunrise, unable to sleep. I had descended the hill again the previous night in a daze, unsure if I had experienced some sort of anxiety dream at its crest. But I knew the circumstances too well to believe that for long. I wanted to contact Julie (the female Mike indicated in his discussion with the creature?) or Steve, but something kept me from it.

I had the strangest feeling that Mike had fully intended me to see everything that I had last night. But to what end? Part of the next Ordeal? To test my trustworthiness—again?

The day itself was dark. Burgeoning thunderclouds had amassed in the night and now threatened rain. I tried writing in my journal, but to no avail.

"So what're your plans for tonight?" my mother asked when I finally came downstairs to search, aimlessly, through the cupboards. She was tending a miniature herb garden that sat in one of the windowsills.

I didn't answer for a moment, pretending to study a can of Campbell's chicken noodle soup. "Oh, maybe going to a party," I finally responded.

"You? A party?" My mother laughed. "When was the last time you went to a party—first grade?"

"Something like that," I said, heading back upstairs with my consolation prize: a box of Triscuits. "Where's Dad?"

"He's at the office again this weekend. They're doing an audit." She frowned, possibly at the stunted basil in the planter. "He'll probably be back late tonight, which means I get to hand out candy. All by myself, if you're going to a *party*." She emphasized the last word and smiled up at him.

"Sorry," I said lamely.

"Don't worry about it. I'll see if Nancy wants to come over and split a bottle of chardonnay." She was thoughtful for a moment. "Why is it that your next-door neighbor seems to always have all the gossip? I mean, they're right *next door*. Wouldn't I basically hear everything that she does?"

I grunted and headed upstairs.

The conversation with my mother had depressed me sufficiently to set the box of Triscuits aside and lay back down in bed. My bedroom walls, covered in horror movie posters and shelves lined with science fiction and fantasy novels, still seemed to work their insulating magic on me. No outside world, no schedule, no goddamned Ordeal tonight...

I awoke with a start in darkness. The sun appeared to be setting; a full moon had arisen on the other horizon, but dark clouds continued to mingle and menace in the distance. Perhaps there would be enough time for trick-or-treaters to amass their fortunes before a truly classic storm hit. I myself had just enough time to get changed and make my way over to the grotto behind the Brake Street house.

I ENDED UP SLOWING down substantially as I walked down to Brake Street—what did I have to lose? They couldn't start without me.

The moon loomed, wildly exaggerated, in the sky; kids in all varieties of Halloween costumes cavorted about, screaming and laughing and racing one another. Tonight I hoped to find out if the mask I wore, Charles Thomas Leland, possessed the level of resolve necessary to survive the weird, messy world that Fear Club was intent on uncovering.

I thought about the Ordeal.

Golem Creek legend held that the Murk had originally been a naturally occurring fissure in the earth, and was once supposedly a functional well. The property surrounding it had been purchased by Laban Black, a wealthy businessman of Welsh ancestry, upon his arrival in America in the eighteen-seventies. Other than constructing an elaborate stone wall around the well itself—doubtless, in part, to keep from having to deal with lawsuits involving people accidentally falling to their deaths within—he hadn't done much of anything else with it.

Laban Black had also built the house on Brake Street, some distance away—the house later occupied by the Flowers family—where he lived a sequestered and quiet life. In a sense, Laban Black had laid the foundation for most of the city of Honorius; in true rich-man fashion, it was his money that silently pulled the strings of politicians as he whiled away his time doing—well, that's what no one was really quite sure of.

The *legend* of Laban Black implied that he'd been "gracefully" kicked out of Wales for some diabolical activities connected with the practice of witchcraft. Everyone had their opinion about it: some people claimed he was a murderer on the level of Bluebeard, others that he had simply engaged in one-too-many affairs with local ladies whose husbands were tired of the intrusions. In the latter case, these affairs were often attributed to some type of ritual magic which the ladies agreed to engage in at his request.

At any rate, the witchcraft connection ended up becoming part of the story behind the "enshrined" wishing well on Chicken Hill. Stories circulated of people in desperate circumstances tossing coins into the well on nights of the full moon, entreating whatever "spirits" dwelt within to answer their prayers. Upon tossing one's coin in, so the story goes, "if nothing you hear, the spirits are near," apparently meaning that your wish would be answered because the coin had been "caught" by a spirit rather than simply hitting the stone basin and echoing.

The oddest part of the entire legend surrounding the well is that, in many cases, *it worked.* Alternative explanations often strained credibility. The story of an old woman whose son had gone off to war, who had subsequently received notice of his death, *with instructions regarding delivery of his body for burial,* made a wish one night at the well. *The very next day,* her son, alive and well, returned home from overseas; everyone, including him, was utterly baffled by the "mistake" made on the part of the army processing service, and due apologies were not long in coming.

There were darker circumstances, too. Other than improbable deaths occurring as a result of vengeance wishes made at the well, stories of "things" occasionally seen coming *out* of the well had been rumored. One man, whose dog had gone missing, sought him one evening in the Murk's environs, and was beset by the presence of "a figure so dark as to be made of black smoke, with great wings like those of a bat's spreading out behind it," holding the dog and retreating into the well's depths. The dog's barking could be heard briefly from within as the man cautiously approached the Murk's edge, then abandoned his search in terror.

All this passed through my mind as I approached the ramshackle property on Brake Street. Someone, probably Steve, had set a jack-o'-lantern glowing in the window of the shed out back. Its fanged teeth leered at me as I stepped inside, thunder rolling distinctly in the distance.

I DIDN'T EVEN BOTHER to concern myself with
the strength of the rope or anything practical like
that. *Just get in and get out,* I thought to myself.
*If there's something down there, whatever the hell
it is, just look it dead in the eyes. Punch it in the
nose if you have to.*

As usual, Mike didn't give me any pointers on
what to do once I got down there.

"Follow your instincts," he said. "The Chaos
Lords will guide you if you are strong."

"And if I'm weak?" I asked, only half in jest.

Mike smiled. "They will guide you if you are
strong," was all he said.

The rope was attached with carabiners to a
harness encircling my torso. Steve patted me on
the back as I got up onto the lip of the well. "Give
'em hell, Charley-boy!" he said confidently. "Er, I
guess, give 'em—something. Whatever."

"Good luck, Charles," Julie chimed in. She lit
two cigarettes and offered me one. I shook my head
and Steve grabbed it from her, taking a huge drag
and inhaling deeply.

"He doesn't need any luck, Julius Caesar!"
Steve asserted. I noted that the T-shirt he wore
under his denim jacket bore the words "FUCK THE
XP" beneath an image of a frowning dwarf holding
a battleaxe.

Mike had retreated a few paces to a small stone
altar set up several feet from the well opening.
"Leave him," he said as he lit two black candles.

Julie and Steve maneuvered themselves beside
Mike.

"*Zod manas zi ba!*" Mike intoned, eyes closed,

hands held out toward the sky. "*Zazas! Zazas! Nasatanada zazas!*" He opened his eyes and gazed at me. I could almost believe that they had become pits of black fire blazing in the midst of his angular, vampiric face.

I saluted once and sidled off the edge, into the darkness below.

THE STORY THAT FASCINATED me the most about old Laban Black was the one about his death.

He had embarked (at the incredible age of eighty-six, no less!) upon what was to be a month-long trip back to his native Wales, ostensibly to oversee the excavation of some ruins once owned by his family. While there, during a visit to the site, a portion of the ruins he had been investigating caved in, causing a general collapse of the old fortress's infrastructure. A complete cave-in ensued, burying Laban alive under several tons of compromised stonework.

"Death by misadventure," one might say. But there were rumors that his death had been precipitated by several individuals who were not at all pleased that Laban had returned to Wales, much less that he perhaps intended to return for good.

His body was never recovered, adding plenty of fuel to the fire of fable surrounding him. His properties in America were promptly swallowed up by several investment firms—all but the properties in and around Golem Creek, which, by some financial trick or other, Laban had managed to make untouchable by any but his closest trusted relative: Mike's great-granduncle, Curwen Flowers.

And so the house on Brake Street was inhabited by several generations of Mike's family, and would be so to this day, had not Mike's own death two years ago prompted an emergency return of his family to England. For whatever reason, the taxes keep getting paid and general upkeep of the house continues, but whether Mike's family will ever inhabit the place again remains to be seen.

That is, of course, if you don't count Mike Flowers himself, whose "cover" is handled (rather deftly, I might add) by the only three people who know that he still exists.

THESE THINGS I THOUGHT or reconsidered as I rappelled down, down, down into darkness.

Mike had allowed me a few items in his untoward grace: a backpack (ostensibly for retrieving any important items I might discover), a miner's flashlight helmet with a spare set of batteries, some strike-anywhere matches, and a compass. I did not intend on remaining down there much longer than it took to (a) realize that it was scary and (b) gather *something* and then tug three times on the rope to have them haul me back up.

It began to rain during my descent—just a light pattering of rain at first, which gradually increased in volume. So far as I knew, water never seemed to accumulate in the Murk—for that, at least, I felt thankful.

About halfway down, I began to notice the echo of my own footfalls against the smooth stone of the interior well wall. The darkness became substantial enough that I decided to pause briefly and turn on the flashlight helmet. A dull, yellowish glow illuminated the mossy stone and blackness beneath me for a radius of about fifteen feet. If anything, the glow actually seemed to make the descent creepier.

Probably got this damned thing the same place he got that air tank for Steve, I thought.

I glanced upward, and paused again briefly. The dull purplish glow of stormclouds delimited by the circular entrance of the well appeared; a brief flash of lightning illuminated the sky, as if to wish me luck.

Or perhaps to say goodbye.

I began to notice small outcroppings of rock from the wall. Some of them had coins on them, old, weatherbeaten pennies, dimes, quarters—I guess the denomination depended upon the degree of importance of your wish. I looked below and noticed that the chasm of the well narrowed somewhat.

Down through the narrowing, I was suddenly beset with an astonishing sight: *someone had spray painted complicated glyphs in various areas of the rock wall.*

I was not only not the first person to perform this act of lunacy, I wasn't even down here for much of a reason at all. Someone else had taken the initiative; someone else had gone ahead and performed the descent, but armed with a means of making their mark—whatever in the world those strange and somewhat unwholesome marks meant.

Who did they intend them to be seen by? Was it something like the weatherproof boxes found at the summits of mountains, containing various messages and the names of those who had gone before?

Or was it, perhaps, something more sinister? A method of "putting a lid" on the Murk, of *keeping something down here*?

I had, I felt, passed a certain point of no return. I began to descend more quickly. Indeed, the glyphs appeared in a ring perhaps thirty feet below surface level, but did not occur again beneath that. A dank smell began to assail my nostrils—where in the world was the floor of the well? It couldn't possibly be much deeper—

At that moment, I hit bottom. More stone and silence met me. I swung my lanterned head about, trying to get a survey of the area.

I was in a room, roughly ovoid in shape, perhaps twenty feet across, with two halls proceeding away from it: one to the west and one to the east. *There were no discernible coins on the floor of the well,* despite the fact that generations of hopeful people had been tossing them hither. *No coins on the floor of the well...sometimes the wishes are answered, if the coins are caught...*

My heart began to beat faster, but I steeled myself. I had been ready for *something* terrifying to happen; I only now realized how much I wished it had been an alligator or whatever.

I turned to my right, to the eastern hall, then to my left. No discernible difference. No markings of any sort, really; just passageways going straight off, as far as I could tell, into blackness in each direction.

How to choose?

I did the unthinkable at that moment. I unhooked the rope from my harness and approached the western hall. Closer inspection showed nothing particularly unusual, nor anything in the way of indicating that the hall curved away beyond twenty or so feet within. The eastern hall entrance proved to look identical to the western one. Breathing in deep, I took a step within the eastern hall entrance, trusting fate—or perhaps Mike's Lords of Chaos—to guide me.

Five steps in...ten steps in...nothing changed. I increased my pace. *There's got to be something down here for me to take back to them,* I thought. Twenty steps in...thirty...

I began to consider turning around and heading back when I heard a distant rumbling coming from the direction behind me. As I turned around to face it, the rumbling became a mild quaking and trembling. As I began to run back to the entrance proper, I was hit with a wall of freezing cold, frothing water that grabbed me like a plaything and pushed me back the direction I had been headed.

I managed to gasp in one or two breaths of air before I went under, sheer panic enveloping me. *Where was it taking me?* I dimly sensed the water beginning to twist this way and that; my body hit the rock walls solidly several times, and I was able to steal a few breaths by desperately pushing myself up toward the ceiling at a few points.

My mind and heart raced. Death by drowning? I'd heard various opinions about it—good, bad, slow, fast? I couldn't remember. As my latest breath began inching its way out of me, the water seemed to slow, and I found myself spilled out onto a smooth stone floor, water streaming away around me. *The lantern had gone out.*

MY FIRST INSTINCT WAS to try to get it working again. I patted the ground around me, happy in the assumption that any noxious creatures would have been washed away in the deluge, at least temporarily. By feel, and carefully, I unlatched the miner's helmet from my head and was able to coax open the small flashlight at its front. I slid out the batteries and placed them in my shirt pocket, then began shaking water out of the lantern itself.

When I could no longer hear water shaking around inside of the flashlight, I re-inserted the batteries, muttered an imprecation against the gods of chance having their way with me again, and switched on the light.

The beam flickered, sputtering somewhat, and finally began to glow dully once again. A chuckle escaped my lips. I placed the helmet back on my head and was about to re-latch it when I saw the loathsome *thing* that squatted across from me in the small cavern I was in, watching me with sickly, yellowish eyes that gazed out from behind long, matted black hair, its body a travesty of humanity, covered in a mossy, dark fur. It lifted one ragged, taloned paw toward its face.

The light went back out.

MOMENTS OF SHEER TERROR and panic were our stock in trade. The Bhairavi Society—so-named after the ancient *yogis* of India, the *bhairavis* or "fearless ones" who had reached levels of awareness beyond all human conception—had instilled in me a great respect for the awesome forces that could be coaxed out of (some) human beings when pushed to the very limits of emotional trauma.

Fear is the great initiator. Without fear, there is no change. Without fear, there is no compulsion for the nervous system to function at a level beyond human squabbling. Let us reach that level of greatness within ourselves, the height that can only be truly found in the deepest, darkest depths...

Mike's words. At that moment in the cavern, I reached a whole new level for sure.

Running would get me nowhere. This was the moment I had been waiting for. Was this one of those things Mike had been conversing with the other night? I had to assume that it had not (yet) attacked me for some very specific reason of its own. *I had to try to take control of this situation.*

"I am here on a mission for Michael Flowers," I spoke as calmly as I could. "Do you know him?"

My voice sounded hollow. It sounded afraid. I heard the thing quivering in the place I had last seen it. I almost said something else, but decided to wait instead; I stood up, staring at the spot where I had seen the creature, pretending that I could see it.

A series of unnatural clicks and gargles followed by an odd hiss of air proceeded from the spot where the thing still, presumably, squatted before me. I recalled that *other* creature during its interaction with Mike, and the fact that it clearly spoke no language that I could discern.

This was going to be more difficult than I

thought.

I assumed that it had responded to me, and took that as a good sign. All things considered, taking it as a *bad* sign would, at any rate, accomplish nothing.

"Bring me the items I am to deliver," I finally decided to say. "And be quick about it!"

I heard it scuffle off. Good? I could still see nothing in the blackness of the cavern; getting out seemed both an imminent concern and far from my thoughts. I took the miner's helmet off once more and tried fixing the lamp again. It flickered briefly, then went right back out. The soaked box of matches in my backpack obviously wouldn't help in the slightest.

I would have to proceed by feel alone. Luckily, the deluge had not appeared to give way to any major divergences on its way here, which implied that if I simply kept my hand on the wall and reversed direction, I should make it back to the well. Provided, of course, there were no further flash floods.

Minutes passed. I became aware of my own breathing, of the closeness of the cavern, of the dampness of my clothing and the oddly invigorating scent of wet stone. Was I supposed to have followed the thing?

I heard shuffling again, then the presence of the creature asserted itself. Something was pressed up against me. A package? The thing clicked and moaned as I took hold of what appeared to be a wooden box of about ten pounds in weight, almost like a cinder block in size.

"I will deliver this promptly," I said. The thing muttered in response, and I decided to add: "I will be sure to tell him that it was *you* who provided it for me."

What I assumed was excited shaking and clicking emanated from the creature. I tucked the box under one arm, then turned quickly and, reaching out a hand to touch the wall to my right, began slowly and surely to pick my way back (I hoped) the direction I had come. Behind me, I heard shuffling and scuttling, then more clicking and moaning from what seemed to be *more than one* creature, fading off into the distance.

Darkness ahead, darkness behind. I wouldn't give in to any sense of accomplishment until I had gotten back to the well.

CONCERN FOR WHAT I prepared to carry out of that dark place began to weigh upon me the farther I walked. As I began to see flashes of lightning appearing up ahead, I knew I approached the well's entrance—but I slowed my pace.

What was in the box?

There appeared to be a simple latch holding it shut. Easy enough to open...

Had Mike said anything at all about delivering *everything* I found? No—"whatever" I delivered would be considered sufficient. *Was this part of the test?*

Something snapped within me. *To hell with it*, I thought, and undid the latch.

Within the box, working solely by touch and the extremely dim light reflected from storm clouds above the well's base, I discerned two items: a small book, about the size of my palm and perhaps half-an-inch in thickness, and an elaborately molded key. The latter felt cold to the touch, and heavy—brass, perhaps, or even silver...

Quickly, unthinkingly—despite my clothes still soaked in flood waters from gods-knew-where—I pocketed the book and key. My pants seemed baggy enough for the items to remain unnoticed—I hoped.

I re-clasped the latch of the box and shoved it in the backpack with the other junk. I re-connected the rope that still hung down into the cavern to my harness. Tugging on the rope, I began to hear bustling above, and in minutes I was being hauled, slowly but surely, back to the surface.

I WAS MISTAKEN TO think that Mike bent forward into the well to help me out. His hands reached just past me and grabbed the backpack, pulling it over my shoulders and retreating with it as I reached the surface, leaving Steve to help haul me over the side of the well, back to the land of the living.

"Proof of success!" Mike uttered as he removed the box from the backpack and gingerly placed it into a large, dry duffel bag of his own. "Charles, you have been judged—and not found wanting!" He clasped his hands together, gazing up toward the full moon above, and began to mutter in some strange tongue under his breath. Steve grinned at me and pulled out his ever-ready whisky flask.

"Water of life," he said, and took a swig before offering it to me. I obliged him, and drained a good deal of it. "Speaking of which, what the hell happened to you down there? It sounded like a fucking deluge. And you're soaking wet."

I shrugged. "Died and came back to life," I said.

Julie laughed and patted me on the back. "I guess we're going back to Mike's for—"

Mike began to chuckle and hefted the duffel bag. "No need," he said. "He has not been found wanting." He headed off into the night, practically bouncing with joy.

I conceded to a slight sensation of guilt. He would get home and find the box empty. He would wonder whether I had opened it, and probably make accusations—which I would stubbornly refuse to acknowledge the truth of, all the while wondering why I had been so stupid to have stolen something whose value I could not possibly conceive. *If Mike ever found out...*

"Looks like we're off the hook tonight," Steve said, gathering up the remainder of the rope as he gazed blankly in the direction Mike had scurried off.

Julie was packing the few other supplies we had brought. "No shit," she said. "What's up with him? He's usually all: 'The Lords of Chaos must be appeased.' Yadda, yadda, yadda." She turned to gaze at me as I rested in the moonlight against the trunk of a tree. She scrunched up her face and feigned mortal terror. "Charley! *What's in the box?!?*"

I laughed. "If you saw what gave it to me, you might not make that joke."

Even Steve paused in his labors at that. Julie

shifted uncomfortably.

I felt unsafe about taking the items home with me. There was only one place I could think of where I might feel anonymous enough to open that book and find out what the hell I had stepped into, and I wanted Steve and Julie with me when I did it.

"You guys want to go to a party?" I said.

JULIE AND STEVE DEPARTED to stash the equipment and then try to swipe some more booze and cigarettes. I headed to my house, ostensibly to change and take a shower, but before arriving there I made a brief detour to our old elementary school, Maple Ridge, a few blocks away. In second grade, I had discovered a loose brick in a corner wall behind one of the dumpsters out back with enough space behind it to house whatever eight-year-old contraband I could get my hands on, e.g., firecrackers, old lighters, a jackknife or two—even a dirt-crusted pack of old playing cards sporting pictures of half-naked women on them, found one day lingering at the edge of oblivion on a gutter grate.

I would stash the book and the key here temporarily, then retrieve them before heading off to Amanda Whitfield's. I thought that, perhaps, an atmosphere of noise and lots of people might somehow diffuse (or, hopefully, *de*fuse) any ill effects associated with their capture and study. In other words, I decided, quite selfishly, that if I was going down, I was going to take down half of Honorius High School with me.

Life's unfair, right?

Maple Ridge was dark, quiet, peaceful. It

alarmed me that, despite what I knew lived below us here in Golem Creek, I felt so resilient, so *unchanged* by the experience of meeting with it. Perhaps Mike was right about us—there was no coincidence in our having been chosen as members of our little "Fear Club." Perhaps also that mere fact itself was the thing that scared me the most.

After locating the correct brick—still there, seemingly untouched even after all these years—I extracted the palm-sized volume and the key. By the light of the moon and a not-too-distant sodium vapor lamp casting an orangish glow over the dim environs, I got a half-decent look at the items.

Thankfully, the book didn't look too terribly damaged after its trek across town in my water-logged pants pocket. Some warping at the edges, but it had a sort of dark leather cover that seemed to be water resistant. Maybe fifty pages bound around with a leather strap, but not even too old-looking—something you could probably buy at a stationery store today.

The key was another matter entirely. It was presumably silver, and probably authentically so, given the tarnish and oxidation—but what a key! It looked both too simple and too complex at the same time; complicated arabesques adorned the handle, and what appeared to be the faces of grinning satyrs or imps peeked out from amongst ornate foliage. The business end looked like the standard "skeleton key" of four bold, ridged teeth, and the whole thing, about four inches in length, seemed to weigh far too much for its modest size.

I stowed the items behind the brick after taking

another quick glance around, then high-tailed it back to my house. I would return here and retrieve them before heading off to the party. I felt a terrible anxiety about having them anywhere near my home. It seemed like a warning that took in more than just the dangers of the creature who had given them to me.

Not to mention the fact that I didn't want the things near me if Mike Flowers were to show up unexpectedly, demanding to know what had become of his treasures. *Why did I feel so certain that he should never have them?*

AMANDA WHITFIELD LIVED IN what most of us would call a "mansion," in a suburb of Honorius called Forty Winks. To get there, you could either take the main road past Cricket River or try to meander through a rather dense thicket of woods, called Foxend because it backed right up to an ancient cemetery called the Foxend Churchyard. I met back up with Julie and Steve at the corner of Brake Street and Main; Julie had deigned to chauffeur us to the party in her glamorous 1981 Honda Civic. Steve, as a gesture toward my position of honor for the night, even allowed me to sit shotgun.

We drove in partial silence, the radio tuned to some alternative station, until Steve decided to interrupt Trent Reznor with the echoing question.

"So," he said. "Um. What's in the box?"

Julie actually started laughing. I hesitated, but couldn't help joining in.

"Come on!" Steve said, laughing now too. "I

know you fucking opened that thing! There's *no way* you didn't open it. Tell!"

I shrugged. "When we get to the party, I'll show you."

Steve gasped, then began acting hysterical, kicking the back of my seat. "I *knew* it! Julie, didn't you know it?"

Julie just kept laughing. Trent seemed unaffected, deep in the world of his own problems.

"A fucking *gold bar*, man! Yes! We cash it in and ditch this place!" Steve concluded. "Why go to the goddamned party? Let's just head to FazMart and have a look!"

FazMart served as the name of an ubiquitous chain of convenience stores located anywhere nature couldn't prevent it from happening.

"I thought the party might be a better idea," I said. "All those people. I mean, what if some *thing* comes looking for it?"

Steve patted me on the shoulder. "Right! Great minds think alike. Take down the high school with you."

Julie's grin seemed plastered to her face, and she chuckled as she lit another cigarette. "It's a good idea. I mean, even if a monster doesn't crash the place, is *Mike* going to show up at the party?"

I hadn't thought of that, but she was right. Mike's single apparent ace-in-the-hole was the assumption, by the rest of the world, that he no longer existed. He was definitely too smart to compromise that.

Then again...

"Then again," I said, "it depends, I guess, on

what he has to lose. Right?"

The chuckling did, in fact, die down a bit at that point.

THE PARTY—WHICH ANNOUNCED itself several blocks before we reached it—provided a perfect mixture of anonymity and distraction. Costumes abounded—everything from your typical "slutty nurse" to a pretty authentic-looking werewolf in what appeared to be John Travolta's *Saturday Night Fever* getup could be found. The "Teen Wolf" had added some post-modernist cleverness to the outfit, adding little devil horns jutting out from the mask. *Rich kids.* The hostess, long-drunk and locked in one of several designer bathrooms on the second floor, was accordingly unable to greet us; we sauntered in unabashed, availed ourselves of a few beers, and forced our way through the throng to locate a secure area for unveiling our spoils.

Molly Furnival was nowhere in sight. Admittedly, this was the first time that *not* seeing her gladdened me somewhat.

Steve suddenly re-appeared near Julie and I.

"This way," he said, motioning furtively.

Only a few more minutes of jostling through the phalanx of vaguely familiar faces got us to a small, sheltered area around the corner of the back patio, close enough to keep us wary of the pulsing dance music of the party, but far enough for us to maintain our sanity and concentrate. The regular bursts of rain were keeping people rather safely swarmed inside. A light burned above a side-door to the house, illuminating an old iron patio table and four plastic chairs, clearly rejects of the backyard landscaper.

"Let's see it!" Steve said, dragging one of the chairs out and motioning for me to sit.

I did so, pulling the small book and key out of the inside pocket of my jacket and placing them on the table. Appropriately timed, the music inside seemed to reach some sort of crescendo, and there was a general eruption of applause and shouting. Steve reached out to examine the key and then, oddly, placed it back on the table with scarcely a comment.

With Steve and Julie both hovering intently over my shoulder, I opened the book to page one. It was clear that there had been a page previous to this one, but that it had been carefully (if imperfectly) torn out. What we saw appeared to be a journal entry, but it read like a short story, which I began to read somewhat hesitantly aloud.

27 Dec. Broken-hearted, banished to this strange tavern in a weird corner of this world, by the light of a dying fire, I drank the potion that would salve the wound.

It was a desperate attempt, and doomed to fail; yet, who would say that this failure was not in every way the longed-for success?

For as I became attuned more clearly to my surroundings, and the strains of some ungodly music wended their way through the porches of my ears, I was alerted to the unconscionable admonition: tonight, of all nights, the bar would close, and alone I would again drift, a ghost of my former self, emptied of purpose, the glorious unnamable Lady whom I had lost no longer part of the home I could not bear to return to.

I paid in cash. Some part of me, at least, had kept the drinking to a minimum tonight. When I stood, the familiar wobble greeted me, and I knew that I could at least stagger to bed. At least.

"It's cold out there. Don't forget your jacket."

I couldn't quite formulate a response, but decided it sounded like good advice. My jacket donned, I proceeded to impress myself by smoothly exiting the building without stumbling into anything or anyone. At least, not that I remembered.

And it was cold outside.

A drizzling rain had begun, and the sidewalks slick with fallen leaves proved something of a hazard to navigate. I lived a few blocks away from grounds, equally a few blocks from the bar right next to grounds, but I would have to pass through part of the quadrangle to reach home. A few cars splashed by. I walked slowly, despite the chill, despite the rain, still warmed by whisky, still wanting to delay the inevitable.

My hesitation managed to get me into trouble soon enough. Through maleficence extraordinary, the rain picked up, along with a blast of cold air sufficient to waken me to my predicament. I had gone the wrong way. I glanced at my surrounds: dark sidewalk, dark overhanging branches of poplar (or was it ash? The death-tree that rewarded acts of great hubris?), a great building whose brick, reminiscent of nothing, crawled with vines like tendrils of dark lightning, each leaf an initiate of the evening's mysteries as they unfurled before me...

One Light.

I proceeded toward it, a wizened single eye of hoary hope. Angled awkwardly above a door of some forgotten wood, chipped and gnarled, I proceeded toward that Light as the storm around me grew increasingly ferocious. Down a small incline laden with unkempt grass, down to the hollow on the side of the building I could not name in my present stupor. On either side of the door rose small hillocks that may once have been an attempt at ornament, but now served the purpose of a degree of shelter from the wind.

The Light flickered as I reached it, and I somehow instinctively knew that I had but little time to waste. The handle on the door felt like ice, and I could sense some intricate carving upon it, the tail of some beast, perhaps, or more tendrils of ivy set in brass. At this distance, I could now discern a small plaque set into the middle of the door, which appeared constructed of a heavier wood than I at first imagined. The letters appeared in bas-relief, and I touched them briefly with one trembling hand before a blast of chill wind purposed to decide my fate. One word was indicated on that door, as icy as the wind itself:

"TRAP."

I opened the door.

I soon acclimated to the dimness that met me. Outside, the wind continued to howl, and I could hear the swooning and mourning of ancient trees muffled by the strange hall I found myself in.

Lit by what appeared to be similar twenty-watt yellow bulbs in ornate, but poorly kept, sconces to either side appearing every ten feet or so, the hall seemed more like a rectangular passageway cut into the side of a mountain than the back entrance to one of the older buildings on grounds. A stone floor, neat and clean considering its obvious age and stage of use, led straight on for perhaps fifty feet. No doors or furnishings appeared to either side, and the wall itself appeared carved out of the same stone.

Briefly, I considered waiting out the heart of the storm here in the entranceway. Whisky and the immediate aversion *of danger had teamed to impel me forward, however, and I started forth toward the end of the hall, the sounds of the storm outside gradually descending into an uncanny silence.*

Upon reaching the end of the hall, I discovered—besides similar paths continuing to either side—another plaque set into the wall. A message appeared in roman-style characters; but what gibberish was this?

After making one or two attempts to read the peculiar sequences of characters that followed, I simply tilted the book so that Julie and Steve could clearly see it:

Dobbsfkdq, Aetoibq!
Webk ylu atk obtp sefq,
rb quob sl dbs seb hby
lk seb lsebo qfpb lc sefq
jbqqtdb.
MQ: Qlooy clo seb ritah byb!

Steve snorted. "So obvious," he said. I continued reading aloud.

And at that moment, I heard the sound of a woman's scream from some distance down the left-hand path. I froze— and immediately relaxed, as laughter followed it, then cheers. Sounds of general revelry ensued. A frat party, perhaps? Had I just stumbled upon one of those fraternity "secrets"?

Undaunted now, I immediately turned to the left and proceeded toward the sounds, which grew louder. At the end of the hall, a simple wooden door inlaid with frosted glass betrayed light and sound and general warmth on the other side of it. With the intention of simply asking for directions—and perhaps scoring a few more drinks—I reached for the door handle—

—and the door opened inward before I could reach it, revealing the most astonishingly lovely woman I had ever seen.

"Charles?!?" she practically shrieked. Clearly, this was the woman who had screamed earlier. Lovely tresses of black hair, so dark it appeared a deep blue in the hazy light, framed an oval face of pale beauty, like a splendid treasure sunk deep in the folds of night.

"I—uh—" Suddenly, it hit me, although its sheer impossibility had functioned to deaden my mind momentarily—it was my beloved, my grace, my light in this dark world! She grabbed me by the lapels of my still-soaked overcoat and yanked me toward her. Breath like strawberry licorice draped a veil of enchanted immediacy over my actions, and I kissed her on the spot.

It was not entirely unwelcome, judging by her response. Unfortunately, it took her aback somewhat; as she began to return my advance, she suddenly became wary of what she did, and thrust me away. I slipped, twisted oddly, and spun about, at which point two further meetings occurred, viz., my right eye was introduced to the door handle behind me and my body to the floor in a heap.

She gasped, immediately descending upon me in a flurry of concern. I suddenly became aware of other partygoers gathering around my most recent absurdity. Oh, merciful Zeus, what had I done now?

"Charles! Oh, love, what have you done to yourself?" I must have blacked out momentarily, for she gently patted my face with fingers soft as angelfeathers. Noise of general confusion arose.

"The man's clearly tanked," said one male voice. I could discern him above me, to the right. He held a cigarette in one *hand and a glass of something as expensive as his clothing in the other.*

I waved my hand above me in what I hoped was a gesture of unconcern. "Long live the king," I said. Several people laughed, and the group began to disperse.

"You've simply massacred yourself, Charles!" This from the Aphrodite still fawning over me. "I'm so terribly sorry! This is all my fault—all my fault!"

"Give him some room for blame, Molly," said the man, still standing as disinterestedly as a telephone pole. "He may want to end up with something for all of this."

"Okay—*what?!?*" This came from Julie, although all three of us were thinking it. "That's fucking *weird*, man. How the hell—"

"Keep reading," Steve insisted, patting me on the shoulder and taking out his flask. I swiped it from him and took a long swig, then handed it back and continued.

"Oh, but he's swelling up!" My Muse, my Saviouress, Molly, gingerly prodded my blackening right eye. "Go get me some ice, Finnegan, before it's too late."

Finnegan audibly sighed, hesitated purposefully, then disappeared from view. Molly somehow contrived to place my head in her lap.

"I'd no idea you knew about this place!" Molly said, sounding delighted. "And tonight of all nights! When did they contact you? Was it the Midsummer Revelry? Oh, it was, wasn't it!"

My depth perception minimized by sight through a single eye, Molly appeared as the central figure in a canvas intended to represent the Ideal of Heaven. I attempted to formulate words, some means of maintaining this state forever. A peculiar shade of memory suddenly invaded my mind like cognac in my nostrils. "The door? There was a door. And a book? I got turned around—"

"Finnegan!" Molly shrieked, looking up. "Where on Earth are you?"

"No, wait! I was, um, in that hallway with the strange sign, the sign written in gibberish—"

"Sign? Oh, right, that sign—wish Roland could've come up with something more clever—"

A crash suddenly resounded through the room. Molly sat up straight, looking concerned. I tried to alter my position to see, and that's when the extraordinary thing happened, more incredible even than the events so far, those gigantic, black, clawed hands wrapped around Molly and dragged her from me—

"Hey, Charley! I didn't know you were here!"

All three of us jumped. I literally fell out of my chair.

"Charley?" It was Molly Furnival. *The same Molly in the book?*

I shoved the book unceremoniously into my coat pocket and lifted out a hand for help. As Julie assisted me in getting up, I noticed Steve surreptitiously grab the key, then smile widely at Molly. "Hey, Molly," he said, waving.

"Molly! Hey—" I started.

"What are you guys *doing* out here? It's *cold*!"

Julie raised an eyebrow and stepped aside to engage another cigarette.

"Yeah, well, I—"

"How's the party in there?" Steve asked. "Anyone dead yet?"

Molly shook her head at him, then put her hand on my arm. The universe melted. "Are you all right?"

"I'm fine!" I shouted. She flinched. "I mean: I'm fine." Not even the fires of imminent death could melt away the inner nerd.

"So, uh," she continued, "what *are* you guys doing out here?"

"Oh, you know, just—you know, we were just—" I stammered.

"—getting ready to come inside and do some *break*dancin', honey, you know? Hey, you wanna find me some girl that's been real liquored up?" Steve did a breakaway move, then spun around and grabbed Julie around the waist. "Wait! No need. I got one *right here*!"

Julie shoved him aside and stalked toward the party, smoke billowing out of her nose like a dragon. Steve followed her, uttering apologies that began sounding like come-ons as they faded into the crowd.

"So, do you want to come inside?" Molly asked, smiling.

"Sure. Of course," I said. We linked arms and started back toward the house, which seemed to have calmed down just a bit.

That is, until the screams started.

When you see your first, real-life werewolf (or whatever the fuck that strange creature was) actually in the midst of its natural, predatory activities, be sure to let me know your reaction. Despite my excellent training by Mike Flowers, mine resembled a strange sort of "falling" sensation, as if my body had dropped to the ground as I remained standing, coupled with spontaneous tearing-up at the eyes.

I stood there, riveted. I felt Molly pull at me once or twice, attempting to drag me away from the incredible scene of gore.

But I was immune to her, to physics, to life. I could only stare.

Before me and, as far as I could tell, *dancing like John Travolta* as the Bee-Gees blasted from the sound system, was the "wolfman" I had seen earlier, whose convincing costume I had taken notice of. Blood and gore covered the white suit; the creature writhed and danced with half of his partner, the upper half, out of which entrails pooled onto the floor beneath him.

He lifted up his head and howled. I saw now that the creature's mask had been *make-up covering its actual demonic visage.* He turned his yellow, ravenous eyes toward me.

"*The sacrifices must be made!*" he growled, dropping his dance partner and pointing one long, black-clawed, wolfish finger at me. "*The Black God returns!*"

Once again he howled, then spun about expertly, performed a further variation on Travolta's *Saturday Night Fever* theme, and proceeded to bound off at an astonishing pace, utilizing an anthropoid-lupine lope, directly into and through the remaining crowd of fleeing partygoers.

Molly was gone.

My trance broken somewhat, I reacted to the sound of several individuals behind me. They were four, scrabbling over the fence, half-climbing and half-falling.

"Did you see it? *Did you see it?*" This from the shortest of them, with hair practically half the length of his body. It took me a moment to realize that the question was directed toward me.

I merely pointed in the direction it had run. They appeared to be scraggly young men, but I didn't recognize them—certainly, with their long beards and hair, they were *not* students at Honorius.

One of them stopped briefly, aiming what appeared to be a video camera in the general direction that the creature had gone.

"Make sure the fucking thing's *on* this time!" yelled the long-haired one. "We can't stop here long! Hey, man," he turned back to me. "You got any smokes?"

I shook my head, but he seemed to have already forgotten his question. "Let's *move*!" he yelled, and ran past me.

I could hear one of the others speak through labored breaths as they resumed their course. "Goddamn it! Did you get that?"

The one with the video camera was already running and filming. The last of them—who could have been the cameraman's brother, but sported a tremendous black beard—paused briefly as he passed.

"Don't worry. I've got this whole thing under control." He patted me on the shoulder and then ran off, screaming something like: "Finally! It's finally *happening*!"

Not knowing what further I could do, I simply sat on the ground, gazing at the incredible scene of massacre laid out before me.

"What the hell are you doing?" Steve appeared out of nowhere. "Get the fuck *up*, man! The cops will be here any minute!"

RAIN BEATING AGAINST WINDOWS. The occasional street lamp.

I found myself lying down, crammed in the back seat of Julie's Honda. I heard Steve speaking from the passenger seat.

"...you see, that I seemed to have stumbled upon a *key* to the whole mystery. A solution. A *means of escape*—"

I could discern that Steve was reading from the journal using a penlight. I groaned.

"Charley?" Steve turned to look at me. "Thanks for not weighing a million pounds. I had to drag your ass out of that shitstorm."

"Huh?"

"You passed out," Julie explained.

"Shit *yeah* you passed out," Steve said. "That was un-fucking-be*liev*able! I mean, come *on*! A *were*wolf? Fucking classic."

A sense of panic immediately assailed me. "I don't know if that was—" I started, recalling the scene. "What about—"

"I got the damned key, dude. We're good. And this book—holy *shit* man, you've gotta keep reading this—"

"No! Not the key. I know that. *Molly*!"

"Oh," Steve said.

"Oh, yeah," Julie chimed in.

I groaned again.

"She's probably fine?" Steve offered. "Right?"

I leaned my head back and closed my eyes. "Right," I agreed.

"I mean, those guys were chasing the thing—" Julie started.

"Oh, hell, *yeah*!" Steve broke in. "Was that not awesome? Monster hunters! *They* were chasing *it*! That's kind of like Fear Club, you know?"

I sat up in the back seat and gazed out the window. "Where are we?"

"Somewhere way out on 101st Street," Julie said. "I think."

"We need to find a new HQ and get to figuring this whole thing out," Steve said. "It looks like 'Charley' wrote us out a map of some sort, but what he's implying is just crazy wild."

I rubbed my eyes. The adrenaline was starting to take its toll on me. "How far did you get?"

"Skimmed a little, but read most of what's here. About halfway through it goes blank. This guy basically admits that he had tried to win back this 'Lady' of his using magic from an old grimoire, but something must have gone wrong—or maybe something went *right*, after all, because he ended up stuck in a dream world where the probabilities were all skewed and time was no longer very linear."

"So is that what the beginning was about?"

"Yeah, I guess. He just kind of dives in—we actually don't know very much about him except that he's a grad student at a school that used to be here in town."

"Except there wasn't ever a university here in Golem Creek," Julie reminded us.

"Right!" Steve said. "But—hey, Jules, pull into that turn-off lane there, with the light."

Julie slowed down the car and turned gingerly into a gravel embankment with a low-hanging light hanging over it from a telephone pole.

"Look at this," Steve said, and extracted a folded sheet of paper from a pocket in the back of the journal. "It's a fucking *map*, man! Can you guess of what?"

I unfolded the page and played over it with the penlight. It was a reasonably good sketch of a city bounded by several hills, with a few labels here and there. *F.C.* written over a couple of little gravestones; *C.H.* by the foothill at one end of town; *H.H.* by a small cluster of buildings at the other end of town. A neatly shimmering circle near another cluster of buildings caught my eye— it had an arrow pointing at it labeled *T.*—but I was distracted immediately by something else. Near the center, an anomaly: what looked like a large, shaded triangle surrounded by a few concentric circles, with a little arrow pointing at it and the initials "*L.B.*"

Despite the odd structures and some of the labels, one thing seemed pretty certain.

"It's Golem Creek," I said.

Steve clapped his hands together and cheered. "Bravo!"

"So our only remaining question," Julie said,

putting the car in gear and heading back onto the road, "is, basically, what the fuck?"

WE FOUND A FAZMART where we could actually stop and plan out our next move, not to mention refuel the car and get something to eat. I was getting a headache and desperately needed some caffeine.

"Put ten dollars in the tank. Stevie Wonder's gotcha," Steve said, getting out of the car and heading into the brightly lit, brick building with its garish red sign. I got out of the back seat and stretched my legs.

"Does he know that Stevie Wonder's blind?" Julie asked, sighing. She hefted the gas nozzle and angled it into the tank. "I still think it's just a *little* suspicious that three of the names mentioned in that book are shared by three people we know," she said.

I stopped short. "Wait. Three?"

"Yeah," she said. "You—Charley. Molly, of course. And Finnegan."

"Who the hell is 'Finnegan'?" I asked.

"He's in there buying cigarettes right now," she said, pointing at Steve, who appeared to be haggling with the night-clerk.

"What are you talking about?"

"Stephanos Finnegan Chernowski. Greek, Irish, Polish. I think it's why—"

"I should have known," I interrupted. "Goddamnit. Of course."

I gazed into the sky, astonished, speechless. The moon had become visible again amidst scudding clouds. *And somewhere, out there, where a "were-wolf" is digesting his dinner of human teenager, scotopic devil-creatures are buzzing and clicking, excitedly preparing for some unconscionable "reward" from their undead messiah...*

Steve headed back toward us, loaded down with three bags and three Mega-Size drinks. "Code Red Mountain Dew. We've gotta be *prepared*, dudes!" He set the drinks down on the hood of the car. "And Twinkies, Snickers. What else? Ah!" He handed a pack of Marlboro Reds to Julie.

"You didn't say anything while I was reading the book, Steve," I said.

"What? Why?"

"Your *middle name* is 'Finnegan.' You're acting like—"

"Calm *down*, Chuckie," he said. "I'm figuring it out myself, as we speak. In fact, I think I know what's going to happen next."

Julie and I both looked at him.

"We're going to go right to the source," he said. "Let's go kill Mike for a goddamned change."

OKAY, I HAD TO admit, this was an idea which had been a long time coming. Neither Julie nor I had any good reasons not to take the "fight"—if that's what it was—right back to Mike Flowers and *demand* that he explain what was going on.

"We've been listening to his goddamned cryptic *bullshit* for *years* now," Steve continued. "As far as I can tell, based on what's in that book, I'm guessing that we're more important to all this—whatever it is—than Mike's let on."

"Wait a second, wait a second," Julie said. "We've all seen what Mike's capable of. Plus, isn't he kind of *dead* already? I mean, we actually *don't know* what that guy can *really* do—"

"Not an issue, Jules Verne," Steve interrupted. "Right—he's 'undead.' Which means he *has died*—"

"That's just crazy-person logic, Steve. It's not the same thing *at all*. We saw what he did. And at Foxend—" Julie suddenly stifled herself.

"What was that?" I asked. This was news. "What about Foxend?"

"Yeah, Julie," Steve repeated. "What about Foxend?"

Julie squirmed visibly. "Let's go," she said, opening the car door.

"No *fucking* way!" Steve shouted. Julie paused. "What about Foxend? What the hell do you know that we don't?"

I couldn't imagine ever seeing Julie Evergreen cry—she just wasn't that kind of chick. But a glint of the gas station lights played in her eyes, where it became obvious that she was holding something back. "Please *don't* ask me again—"

"What about *Foxend*, Julie?" Steve said again, a weird grin twisting his face.

I had had enough. "Shut the fuck up, Steve," I said. "Don't be a goddamned sadist."

Steve chuckled, breaking eye contact with Julie. He pulled a Snickers bar out of one of the bags. "Just fucking with you, baby." He opened the car door and got into the back seat. "You can ride shotgun again, Charley. It's your big night, after all!"

I glanced at Julie, who quickly swiped both palms over her eyes and breathed out heavily.

"Maybe we should head back to Brake Street?" I suggested. "Even if we don't exactly *kill* Mike, we might be able to pressure him into telling us *something.*"

"What about the key? The journal?" Julie asked.

"We'll stop by Maple Ridge first," I said. "I know where we can hide them."

Julie nodded, getting back into the car.

"Sorry, Jules," Steve said. He tried to pat her on the shoulder, but she visibly flinched. "Hey, seriously. I'm sorry."

I sat down in the passenger seat. "Let's just chill out, okay? We might officially have done *too much* tonight."

Julie turned the ignition and lit another cigarette. Just then, screeching tires and the strains of some raucous speed-metal band erupted from the darkness beyond the FazMart, followed by the unmistakable sound of an automobile smashing into something.

"What the hell?" I said. Steve started laughing. Julie hung her head briefly, then put the car in gear.

AT THREE IN THE morning, it's easy to wonder which way is up—which was literally true when we came across the shattered remains of an overturned Pontiac 6000 a block away from the FazMart.

Julie slowed the car to a crawl, then stopped, headlights shining on the wreckage. The roads out here well past Forty Winks were dark and untraversed even in daylight, being mostly the "back way" to get out of town without having to pay any tolls.

"What the *fuck*?" Steve was pressed up between Julie and I, straining to see.

"Is there anybody *in* that car?" Julie asked.

I was hesitant to get out, especially given my immediate conviction that there were to be few if any coincidences tonight, but proceeded to undermine my better judgment.

"Steve, you're coming with me," I said. "Julie, just keep the car running."

In moments, Steve and I found ourselves with literal blood on our hands.

"God*damn* it," Steve exclaimed. "We've got to call an ambulance."

Three bodies, none of which appeared to be living, were still seat-belted into the car.

"Are those—" I started.

"Yep. Looks like it," Steve said. "Those are the weirdos from the party. The guys chasing the wolfman."

"I thought there were four of them?" I said.

Steve shrugged.

"Okay," I said. "Let's get back to FazMart and call an amb—"

"Wait a second!" Steve was reaching into the car.

"Dude, what are you doing? I don't think you're supposed to move them. What if someone broke their neck?"

"Oh—*oh*," Steve said. "Nasty. There *are* four bodies in here—mostly."

I cringed. "I'm going to count to *five*, and then I'm *getting the fuck out of here*," I said.

"Check it *out*!" Steve extracted two black canvas bags through the back seat window. "Spoils of war!"

"Steve! For Christ's sake—"

"Right! Let's get the hell out of here."

I hesitated, standing there somewhat blankly as Steve dove back into the Honda. "C'mon, Chuckie! Gotta call an ambulance!"

BACK AT THE CONVENIENCE store, I placed an anonymous call for an ambulance, hoping that there were no hidden cameras surveying the spot. Minutes later we were heading back toward the center of town.

"We've got to regroup," I said. "Now we've got *more* stolen merchandise to deal with."

"This shit is *great*!" Steve was playing his penlight over the contents of the bags.

"Why didn't you stop him?" Julie asked.

I looked over at her. "I know that Steve can hear me. I will ignore that question."

Steve was laughing.

"What is it?" I asked.

"The *camera*, dudes!" Steve was ecstatic. "This is the fucking *video camera*! And it's got the tape in it!"

"Oh my God," Julie said. "That means—"

"We've got footage of that *werewolf*!" Steve finished. "Can you believe it?"

I had to admit to an undeniable sense of accomplishment at Steve's extremely uncouth kleptomania. Actual video footage of a werewolf? Or whatever the hell it was. This was unreal. And who knew what else was on that tape?

My brief moment of illumination fell slightly flat. "Guys," I said. "Who knows what else is on that tape?"

Steve's chuckling faltered. "Oh, yeah," he said. "Right."

"Because now we potentially have a fucking *snuff* film, for Christ's sake," I continued. "That's got to be a federal offense."

"We don't know what's on it," Julie said.

Steve, ever undaunted, took his cue. "This is probably just *X-Files* shit, man. We don't *want* the Feds to have it—what have they ever done for us, anyway?"

"I just hope you didn't get your goddamned fingerprints on anything, Steve," I said.

"No way!" Steve responded. "I'm pretty sure, at least."

I sighed. "Give me one of those cigarettes, Julie."

"Where should I head?" Julie asked, handing me the pack. We were rapidly approaching Golem Creek proper again.

"It's got to be somewhere relatively anonymous," I said. "But somehow not public, either. Any ideas?"

I lit a cigarette. Steve started chuckling again from the back seat, oblivious.

"Oh! Steve, who's that guy you were getting the stuff from?" Julie asked.

"Stuff?" I said.

"Pete's!" Steve exclaimed. "Pete Jarry! 'Best weed in the Shire.'"

"Pete Jarry?" I repeated. "I guess that could work—"

"He's over on Shrub Lane, past the Pizza Hut," Steve said.

"Of course," Julie said. "The drug dealer who lives by the Pizza Hut. Classic."

"Oh, *man*," Steve said. "As if this night couldn't get any *better*!"

"I'd still like to know if Molly's okay—" I started.

"Hey, there's half a carton of Camels in this backpack!" Steve said.

"And, at any rate, it would be nice to know that Mike's not poisoning the town water supply to get at us, you know," I said.

"There's at *least* five dead people as of this moment," Julie said. "The guys in the car crash. Whoever got *eaten* at Amanda Whitfield's party."

"Horror novels?" Steve said. "What's this— *Bloodcurdling Tales of Horror*... Oh! Lovecraft. Hell, yeah."

"There's horror novels in that bag?" I asked.

"Yep," Steve said. "Oh, not just that! *Reign in Blood* on cassette. Slayer! Two cans of spray paint." He lifted one out and shook it. "Empty. Heavy metal, vandalism, werewolves, H. P. Lovecraft— it's too bad those guys are dead. I could've partied with them."

"We *all* could have," I said. "Jesus, who *were* those guys?"

"You'll like this, Charley," Steve said, and patted me on the shoulder. "Check it out."

He handed me a spiral-bound notebook. "Don't tell me," I said. "Another journal?"

Steve started laughing again.

"Hand me that tape," Julie said. "I need a soundtrack."

WE ROLLED INTO PETE Jarry's neighborhood about twenty minutes later. Pete lived in one of those weird neighborhoods that stopped being built in the '70s, where every house was slightly different because most of the architects were presumably doing acid on a regular basis. Jack-o'-lanterns still burned on the porches of some of the houses; Halloween decorations fluttering in a light breeze lent an air of horror-movie eeriness to the whole scene. Julie had to rely on Steve's dim memory of monuments to pinpoint the right place, but after "the second stone fountain with a mermaid" and "the green house—no, the yellow one with the tree that looks like an afro," we finally parked in a bank of shadows by Pete's house and turned off the car.

Everything seemed a bit *too* quiet. The light chirping of crickets and trickling of yet another stone fountain (was that a thing thirty years ago?) combined to diminish further the silence following Slayer's frantic guitar riffs.

"Steve...?" I said.

"Yeah, hang on, let me out," Steve said.

I scooted the seat forward. Steve slid out of the car and scampered past a dim yellow porch light, into the darkness behind Pete's house.

Julie and I waited in silence for a moment.

"That fucking guy," Julie said.

"Tell me about it," I said.

"You love him, you hate him," she continued.

"I don't know," I said. "Mostly hate him?"

"I don't know," Julie said.

"Truth be told, *I* wouldn't have stolen that camera," I said. "Does that make me a pussy?"

Julie snorted. "None of us are pussies," she said. "Not after all of Mike's bullshit."

I shifted uncomfortably in my seat. "So..."

"There was this thing, down under one of the mausoleums."

"What?"

"In Foxend Churchyard."

"Oh." I said. Revelation time. But why to me? Why now? Steve was likely to be back any minute.

Julie sighed heavily. "I'm not supposed to say anything—"

"Hey," I rested one hand lightly on her shoulder, half-hoping that she *wouldn't* say anything. I had to stifle an urge from the other half of me to *beg* her for the info. "Hey. You don't have to. Whatever helps."

Julie smiled, gazing down at the steering wheel, and patted my hand with one of hers. "I don't know if Mike's full of shit or not about this. He said I couldn't tell *anyone* about it. Not anyone. He said one of us would die for real if I said anything."

I recalled her mentioning this to me, of course. But after having stolen the goods effectively right out from under Mike's nose earlier this evening, I was less inclined to assume our safety. Five dead bodies tonight...*so far...*

"So he had me take off all my clothes—"

Nope. Didn't want to hear it. "Oh, shit, Julie, please don't tell me this—"

"He wasn't watching, or anything," she continued. She was going to do it. I gazed toward Pete's in desperation. *Come on, Steve!* Please *butt in like you always do!* "He had me put on this white silk gown." She paused, briefly. "Then he gave me a knife, like a ritual dagger, or something. Big knife."

She was sniffling at this point. "Big knife," she said again. "He says to me: 'Go into the darkness, love. Don't hesitate.'" She paused. I wanted to remove my hand from her shoulder, but she wouldn't let it go. She looked up at me.

"How much darker could it get?" she asked me.

I realized that she was basically re-living whatever trauma Mike had forced upon her, right in front of me. My only interest was in escaping at that moment. I continued to pray secretly for Steve to *get the hell back*—

"Whatever it was," she said, "I killed it."

I started. "You—killed it?" I said stupidly. "What do you mean?"

"It sounded like...like..." she struggled to get it out. Tears were bursting out of her eyes. She turned and looked at me, and my heart sank; I'd never seen anything so pitiful before. "It sounded like a little *girl*, Charley. It sounded like a little *girl.*" She broke down completely. "But I couldn't *see* anything. I couldn't *see*. Just blood. Just blood all over me. Afterward."

Julie collapsed into me, sobbing uncontrollably.

I admit I had no practice with this sort of thing. Patting her on the head seemed stupid, not quite enough. But trying to make out with her would be seriously crossing the line, obviously. I felt miserably inadequate, and opted to simply freeze while she got it out of her system.

Thankfully, Julie broke free of me moments later. "I'm sorry," she said, opening the glovebox and grabbing a handful of old Taco Bell napkins. She blew her nose. "Oh, Jesus. Christ. I'm sorry. Please don't—um—"

"Don't—ah—don't worry. Seriously," I said, relief washing over me, despite the extremely disturbing burden I now carried with knowledge of her Ordeal. "Not a soul."

She blew her nose again and looked over at me. Then she laughed.

"What?" I said, taken aback. "What the fuck?"

"You've got snot, all over your jacket," she said, laughing. "Jesus Christ, I'm sorry, Charley." She reached over with some of the napkins and succeeded in smearing them over the mess. "Oh, shit. Man."

"Just—" I took the napkins. "Let me. Don't worry about it."

A scuffling sound from the side of Pete's house alerted us to someone's presence. Steve emerged from the shadows, grinning from ear to ear. He beckoned us over with one hand, then took a drag off of what was obviously a very fat marijuana cigarette, smoke billowing out of his nostrils into the early morning air.

PETE JARRY'S DEN WAS exactly what I suspected it would be: a pothead paradise. Besides having no discernible flat surfaces other than the floor, walls, and ceiling, the most prominent sources of illumination came from an ancient stereo receiver and fat, multicolored candles in holders located variously throughout the room.

He lived in the basement of his parents' house, accessed by way of an external set of doors and a set of stone steps located around back. Access to the house itself lay at the other end of the rather large room, up a flight of wooden stairs.

"We're lucky," Steve said as he led us around. "He just got back thirty minutes ago."

"Where was he?" I asked.

"Doing *drug dealer* stuff, of course!" Steve hissed.

Pete was smiling gratuitously, gazing at us from his position in an oversized red-and-white bean bag chair. An enormous glass bong sat poised between his legs. "I'm glad you guys came," Pete said, once we had all assembled. "I was really starting to wonder if Halloween was just going to, like, you know, end."

I smiled at him. Pete was a good guy, as far as I knew, even if he did seem a little (as he would put it) far out.

"You really don't mind if we crash here?" Steve asked, idly flipping through the pages of a record catalog.

Pete was hitting the bong for all he was worth, but managed to shake his head. "No, dude," he breathed hesitantly, smoke trickling out of his nose and mouth. "Totally cool. Good to see you again, Charley. You'll have to tell me how it went."

I looked back and forth between Julie and Steve in bewilderment. Julie grinned at the druggie time-slip; Steve just shrugged. Blowing out the remainder of the smoke, Pete angled the bong toward Julie. "Who are you, again?"

Julie shook her head politely. "No, thanks. Julie. Evergreen."

He nodded. "Smoke?" He angled the bong toward me.

"I'm good, thanks," I said. "Hey, didn't you have something you were trying to tell me the other day?"

Pete shrugged and raised his eyebrows. "Did I?" He thought for a moment. "Oh, *right*! That Voynich shit—wasn't that from Stek?"

Julie peered at me, silently mouthing, *Voynich shit?*

"It's somewhere around here—" He cut himself off, waving with one hand and lifting his lighter with the other.

I figured we'd try to make use of our time while Pete oriented his present self with his past. "Do you have a TV set? With a VCR?" I asked.

Pete was hitting the bong again, apparently having already forgotten his task. "Sure thing, dude. Over there, behind the altar."

The "altar" was apparently an octagonal table placed almost centrally in the room. Upon it, reverently disposed, stood a miniature replica of an Easter Island head, carved out of dark, heavy wood. Some cheap-looking trinkets and little metal amulets surrounded it. Barely visible behind drapery decked out in Tibetan *senzar* characters was an old TV set framed in a great wooden box.

I grabbed the video camera bag and made my way over to it. "Does this thing work?" I asked.

Pete nodded.

"Oh, shit, I've *gotta* see this!" Steve said, suddenly interested. Julie had joined me over by the TV, and we were both attempting to figure out how to connect the various wires to the video camera.

"What'd you guys film?" Pete asked from behind me. "Did you guys make, like, a horror movie or something? That would be awesome."

"You're not worried that he's going to snitch?" Julie whispered to me as we tried to separate out the various connecting wires.

I glanced back behind me. Pete was leaning back in his bean bag chair, eyes closed.

"I'm not worried," I said. "Steve, does this thing go here?" I indicated one of the wires.

Steve grinned and proceeded to connect the device up to the TV set without another word. I turned the knob in front to "ON," and gradually the "Channel 3" white noise appeared on the screen.

"Rewind it," I said. "I want to see whatever they shot from the beginning."

GRAINY, POORLY SHOT, POORLY lit, and utterly amazing: these words best describe the strangely magnificent video that the impulsive, chaotic-neutral Steve Chernowski thieved from the wreckage of those Four Horsemen of Golem Creek's mundane apocalypse—may the gods of rock 'n' roll have mercy on their souls.

"I want to see it again," Julie said. Pete Jarry was out like a light, and there didn't appear to be any movement or hint of interruption from any other part of the household. So we re-watched it—all twenty-seven minutes of it, and were not less astounded after reviewing the material.

FIRST, THE TYPICAL BLACKNESS and banging around you get from someone trying to get a video camera focused and recording. Voices from off-camera: "Is it going? Is it going?" All that stuff.

The strangeness, however, begins almost immediately: someone is training the camera on what at first glance appears to be a puddle of water in near-darkness with some light glinting off of it. A voice: "Are you getting it?" An affirmative grunt. "Make sure you get the edges. Swing around so we get the whole thing."

It's then that you realize the shimmering puddle is *vertical*—it's not a puddle on the ground. The camera moves to reveal in a swathe of dim light what appears to be an underground cavern, or a basement filled with all sorts of rubble—broken chairs and what look to be shattered mirrors, perhaps the remains of a table and some shelves. Then it's back to the shimmering puddle, where it steadies.

"Okay," a voice says off-camera. "Whenever you're ready."

A dark-clad figure emerges from the right and stands before the puddle. From the general appearance, although you don't see his face, it appears to be one of the four monster hunters. "Now?" he says.

"Go for it," the off-camera voice says. And then the figure steps into the puddle and *disappears*. As if predicting the disbelief of whomever might be watching in the future, the cameraman subsequently approaches one edge of the puddle and proceeds to walk *around* it, revealing that the puddle possesses no depth at all—it looks exactly the same from behind as it does in front.

Next, filmed from one edge of the puddle, we watch what is now obviously the second of the monster hunters walk into the puddle. He steps toward it, steps *into* it, then also disappears into it, just like a magician's trick—except infinitely better.

Finally, a third guy goes in. The cameraman then speaks: "Here goes nothing." He approaches the puddle and, from the perspective of the camera itself, we step through...

...*into a completely different environment.* It's another underground room, but this one is immaculately clean. The other three are there, happily chatting with each other. They break into applause when the cameraman comes through.

"Who's got the beer?" the cameraman says mockingly.

Another voice: "Let's head up."

We follow them up a dark flight of stairs and through a heavy-looking door, into what appears to be an abandoned storage shed. Moonlight shines into the room from a couple of grimy, barred win-

dows set high up near the ceiling. Someone undoes
a chain and padlock from another door, this one of
corrugated tin, at the other end of the room. The
whole group exits into a forest at this point, and
the camera blacks out for a moment.

STEVE PAUSED THE VIDEO.

"That's *got* to be the tin shed on Old Man
Plunkett's land, on the far side of Chicken Hill,"
Steve said.

"Might as well be," I said. "No one I know has
ever been in there. Plus, they get to the wishing
well right after this."

"Doesn't Max Plunkett basically wait outside
his house with a gun every night?" Julie said. "I
heard that's how Chris Baxter actually got that
bullet wound."

Chris Baxter was a local kid who apparently
got drunk one night and ran through Max Plunkett's land on a dare. The story varied: either Max
Plunkett shot him, or he shot himself in his stupor,
and blamed it on Max Plunkett.

"Maybe they know him? Max Plunkett, I mean,"
I suggested.

Steve re-started the video. There it was again:
shaky camera trudging through woods—and then
the revelation. *One of the creatures from the wishing well*, loping through the forest by moonlight.
The scene was quite terrifying; the cameraman and
his three cohorts understandably stayed back quite
a ways.

The creature disappears briefly, and the next
thing we know, we're watching through the wind-

shield of a car.

"—can't believe we lost it!" one of the guys is saying. "What's that up ahead?"

They were clearly near Amanda Whitfield's at this point. And suddenly we see it: the bat-winged creature descending from dark sky onto the Whitfield residence roof. Excited clamor of voices—the car stops, and the four get out. You can't make out much from this point until they clamber over a fence and the cameraman pauses briefly to take a shot of the creature flying off toward a patch of forest. Screams erupt, and the camera swings over to take in the Travolta werewolf pulling his dance moves.

"Goddamn it! Did you get that?" we hear off-camera. This part was obviously when they were right next to us. The familiar shouts and encouragements of the monster hunters follows, over screaming and blaring party music. Then blackness, one final scene indicating the bat-winged creature evading the camera's viewpoint.

THANKFULLY, THE CAMERAMAN SEEMED so intent on keeping the monsters in sight, he never caught any of us on video.

"So, what this means is—" I started.

"They weren't following the werewolf," Julie finished. "It was that *other* thing. Charley, was that what you—"

"Yes," I said. Steve let out a low whistle. "It was. So that was it. They were following something else, like the thing I saw in the Murk, and they *happened upon* the thing at the party. What kind of a fucking coincidence is that?"

"It's not coincidence," Steve said. "No way. Too weird."

"No, it's *not* a coincidence. We still have that journal to account for. We don't know what that key unlocks. And this—" I said, rummaging through the backpack. "This other notebook."

Steve was unhooking the video camera from the TV set. I flipped open the journal and riffled through it: entries written in pen, dated. Sketches— it looked like maps, blueprints.

Julie gazed at it over my shoulder. "We should probably get out of here before Pete wakes up," she said. "We can stash this stuff."

"Stash it here," Steve said.

"Is that a good idea?" I asked.

"It doesn't look like he cleans up very often," Julie said. "We can probably put it over there." She indicated a half-open closet next to the TV set. Old board games and clothes spilled out onto the shag carpet.

"Plus, he may not even remember us coming over," Steve said.

I wasn't too sure about it, but I didn't quite know what else to suggest. We couldn't fit it all behind the brick at Maple Ridge. This place was about as random as we could hope for.

"Can we get back in?" I asked. "I mean, whenever we need to?"

"Sure," Steve said. He pulled a house key out of his pocket and waved it at me.

"Did you *steal* that?" I said.

"Sure," Steve answered. "Gotta have insurance."

I frowned at him.

"What?" he said. "It was just *sitting* there!"

"But where do we go from here?" Julie asked.

"I already *told* you guys," Steve said. "We're going to *Mike's*. We're gonna go *kill* that fucker— or at least see if we can get him to fess up to something."

I glanced over at Julie and shrugged. "Nothing to lose?" I said.

"I'm fucking *exhausted*," she said.

"It's all right, Jules," Steve said. "You're just the wheel-man. Charley and I will go rough him up. You're good for that, right, Charley?"

"I don't think I will ever sleep again," I said. "And you're obviously high."

Steve saluted. "Yep," he said.

I grabbed the stuff to bury in the back of Pete's closet.

"I'll go start the car," Julie said, getting up.

That's when we all noticed that Pete was gone.

"A FUCKING *SPY*!" STEVE shouted.

"Keep your voice down!" I whispered harshly.

"I can't believe that a guy with grass that good could be *so bad*!" Steve continued.

The bong rested, looking somehow pleasantly stoned, against the altar. Other than that very slight change, it appeared as if Pete had simply vanished into thin air.

"That guy had to move lightning fast and with complete silence for us to have missed him," Julie said.

Steve was nodding vigorously. "That's in their *training*, Jules!" He started opening up drawers and checking under the mattress.

"Steve, what the *fuck* are you doing? We've got to get out of here," I said.

"He's checking for weed," Julie said.

"Crime of opportunity!" Steve said as he riffled through a fat dictionary on a shelf, presumably checking for a false center. "Except, it's not really a crime, because he's a *spy*!"

"Well, hurry up, man," I said. "Let's just get the hell out."

A bumping sound, coming from the door at the other end of the basement, the one leading up into the house proper, stopped everyone in their tracks.

"Shit!" Julie whispered.

All three of us scrabbled toward the basement stairs. Steve's foot caught in a pile of afghans. A stack of *High Times* magazines and, oddly, *Nasco Scientific* catalogs spewed forth from under them. I grabbed his arm, trying desperately to help him back up—

"You guys don't want tacos?"

We froze. It was, of course, Pete. We turned our heads collectively. He was wearing a bright pink bathrobe over pajamas and holding an enormous plate of what appeared to be the finest collection of Mexican viands the world had ever seen.

He sat back down in his bean bag chair and set the plate on the floor in front of him.

"Help yourself," he said, taking a bite out of a crunchy taco. "Oh, and that video you guys were watching?" he continued, chewing loudly. "I know those dudes. I've smoked those guys out."

We descended like vultures on the tacos—
but this food was no carrion. Absorbing, delicious,
exquisite; all these things I knew no longer as ad-
jectives, but rather as facts in a universe of Pete
Jarry's invention.

Relief, a dastardly mirage, smiled, shook my
hand, and promptly returned me to our quest.

"You saw what we saw?" I asked. Steve reclined
with a glass bottle of Coke from a small refrigerator
hidden elsewhere in the contours of the room, a
look of satisfaction tinged with longing on his face.
Julie appeared moderately peaceful for the first
time all night.

Pete nodded. "Yup. My brother brought them
by." He thought for a moment. "Booker and Staley.
I forgot the other two guys' names."

"Your brother? Stek?" I said. His brother was
rumored to be going insane by the majority of
Honorius High. He worked at one of the FazMarts
in town, and had apparently either seen or been
pursued by a demonic creature one night several
months ago. This notion had blossomed into more
insidious reports concerning Stek's circumstantial
involvement in a number of other grisly events.
Rumor spread like quicksilver, and was just as impossible to hammer down into facts, but everyone
had an opinion on him.

I decided to dive in. "You know that what Stek
saw—"

"Was real. Sure," Pete finished.

"But everyone else thinks—"

"Hey, man, Stek couldn't ever hurt anyone," Pete explained. "He couldn't *ever* have done all that crazy shit. I love him, but I gotta admit the dude's pretty boring, for the most part. When he told me about seeing monsters, I was like, 'Hell, yeah, bro! Now we're gettin' somewhere!'"

"And the guys from the video?" I asked.

"Totally legit," Pete said. "That video's not as interesting as some of the other ones."

Steve and Julie both sat up straight. I fumbled for words.

"You're saying there's *more*?" Steve said.

"Oh, hell, yeah," Pete said. "I mean, I don't know if it all takes place in Golem Creek, but—"

"Where the hell are those guys *from*?" Julie asked, exasperated.

Pete thought for a moment. "I think they said 'Tulsa'? Something like that."

"Where the fuck is 'Tulsa'?" Steve asked. Suddenly, his face lit up. "Did they mean *Tesla*? They're robot creations of Nikola Tesla!"

Pete smiled broadly. "Probably, dude."

"You *did* see them step through that portal, right?" I asked.

Pete nodded. "That's some incredible shit," he commented.

"But did they ever say where it was?" Julie asked.

Pete retreated into his typical pothead moment of reverie. "Chicken Hill, right?" he said.

Steve nodded. "Bingo," he said.

"But that's *really a portal to another world*," I said, the sense of sheer amazement at the situation returning once again.

"We don't know if it's to another world," Julie said. "I mean, what if it's just to another part of *this* world? Like South America, or something."

"I mean, shit," Steve said, "if monsters and stuff exist, why the hell not a portal? I mean, where are they all coming from, anyway?"

"Tulsa, I guess," Julie said.

Pete looked suddenly concerned. "Is that just another word for *hell*, maybe? Do you think those guys are demons? And they call their hell-world 'Tulsa'?" He shuddered. "I can't *believe* I smoked those guys out."

I tried to reassure him. "I don't think those guys are demons, Pete. After all, they were *chasing* monsters, right?"

Pete's look of worried concern vanished. "Right," he said slowly, smiling again. "Right."

Despite the lingering clouds of pot smoke in the air, I was starting to feel anxious again about the entire situation. Had Molly made it home all right? What was Mike Flowers planning next? And should we wait for *him* to contact *us*?

I also realized that the "guys from the video" were all probably *dead*—maybe one or two in critical condition at Golem Creek General Hospital—and that a "wolfman" breaking all the rules of horror-movie conduct was presumably still on the loose.

I was at least pleased that Pete hadn't asked us *where* we got the video itself—

"Those guys are all dead, you know," Steve said.

I breathed out heavily and glared at Steve. He shrugged his shoulders, as if to say, "What?"

"Aren't we all?" Pete said. He grabbed the last of the tacos from the plate and took a large bite. "Mm." He suddenly stopped chewing. "Oh, *man.* Seriously?"

We all sat silently for a moment.

"I totally forgot to put the hot sauce on these. Oh, *man.*" He chewed some more, solemnly. "All those packets, too."

We realized quickly that having a drug dealer for an ally was quite possibly the greatest boon to come our way since—well, since surviving the Ordeals, I guess. If you wanted information about the underworld—literal or otherwise—you needed to know the Hermes, the messenger god, who was constantly dealing with it.

I asked if it would be all right if we stashed some of our things in his closet, and Pete just nodded, smiling. "Dig," he said.

Pete suggested we contact Stek directly if we wanted to know more about "monsters." He jotted down Stek's address on a stray rolling paper, then shifted his attention to the stereo.

"You guys ever listen to Rainbows are Free?" he said. "Dude made me a tape."

After that, he seemed quite content to fall asleep and leave us to see ourselves out.

WE DECIDED BY UNANIMOUS vote to head back to the Brake Street house and face Mike directly, rather than waiting.

The sun had supposedly risen, although you

couldn't tell. Dark clouds massed above, sealing us in. It was like Halloween night was not being allowed to end.

We pulled up to the curb a block away from the Brake Street house, per our usual convention.

"We just go in," I said. "We knock. We go in. We sit down and try to have a civil conversation with him."

"And if he freaks out?" Steve asked.

"We deal with it," I said. "Or run."

"'Or run,'" Julie repeated. "I'll remember that one. Best advice ever."

"Or *die*," Steve said.

"Yeah," Julie said. "But *how*?"

I opened the car door. "Why don't you guys just wait here?" I said. "If I'm not back in five minutes—"

"Hell, no," Steve said. "Right behind you."

Julie got out of the car as well. We proceeded to unfold our total lack of plan—to alleviate our anxiety, if nothing else.

AND I SUPPOSE OUR plan "worked," in a sense, since Michael Flowers was nowhere to be found.

The door was unlocked. When I stepped in, half expecting to be axe-murdered on sight, I initially breathed a sigh of relief at the room's occupancy level: zero. But then a newer, more profound concern overtook me: *where was everything?*

In the center of the room sat the box I had handed Mike, its lid open. But other than that, and some scraps of papers and posters left on the walls, the entirety of the room was *empty*.

"Woah," Steve was the first to announce. "Okay. I didn't expect this."

Julie approached the box and peered cautiously down into it. "You think he was really that pissed?" she said. "He just fucking packed up and *left*?"

I didn't quite know what to make of the situation. Geared up for a fight, I suddenly found myself more tired and confused than ever. "I really, honestly didn't expect this," I said. "An argument, some yelling, possibly. Not *eviction*!"

"Wait a minute," Julie said, leaning closer to the box. "Let's just look at this. There's *got* to be a reason this box is still here."

Steve and I both approached the box and peered inside. "False bottom," Steve said. "You got that stuff out of a false bottom? Clever."

"Oh," I said. That sinking feeling again. "Oh, my God." Two precisely delineated bas-reliefs, fitted for two very precise items: one spot for a palm-sized book, the other for an intricately carved skeleton key...

Julie figured it out instantly. "Oh, shit," she said. "Steve, no. No. He did *not* get those things out of the *false bottom*." Steve raised his eyebrows and took a step back.

"Huh," he said. "Well."

Suddenly, the evening's events began to make sense. A book and a key—fake ones on *top*, real ones on *bottom*... I guess if you knew what you were supposed to be looking for, you'd assume that the first book and key you found in the box were the very things you needed—and you'd be *wrong*.

"Holy shit," Julie said. "Do you realize what

you did, Charley?"

"Yes, Julie," I said, trying to roll some of the tension out of my neck. "I can quite clearly see that I fucked up."

"No offense, but that's exactly right," Julie said. "Because think of it: if you hadn't taken the book and the key out, *he might not have known to check for a false bottom in the box.*"

Steve immediately started laughing. "Ha, *ha*! Now yuh done it, Charley-boy!"

I was too tired to punch him. Not that it would have done any good. It had been proven physically impossible to shut Steve Chernowski the fuck up.

"But, then, what were we reading in the journal?" I said.

"Who the hell *knows*?" Julie said. "Maybe a spell of some sort? Touch the key, read the book, and you suddenly end up in a sort of alternate universe where werewolves in fucking John Travolta getups are killing people?"

I slumped down to the floor, leaning my back against the wall. "I want to go home," I said. "I need to sleep."

"Or Mike, for whatever reason, can't get to the damn box himself," Julie continued, speculating. "So he sends someone *else* to go get it for him. And he *knows* that there's probably a protection spell on the thing! But whoever first opens the box gets hit with it, *leaving* him *to run off with the* real *stuff...*"

"So he knew I was going to open it," I said.

Julie nodded. "A set-up," she said.

And now it *did* make sense: seeing Mike the

night before the Ordeal...his expert assumption that I would feel slightly offended by the whole mess, and want to keep some of the spoils for myself...allowing me plenty of unobserved time to do so...

Once again, I began to wonder if all of the Ordeals were fakes, intended to weave one gigantic illusion over the few people Mike thought capable of actually getting the box for him. But he had to choose the right person—one who would do the work, but whom he could *not* trust entirely, that he could trust *just enough...*

"Steve," I said. "What would you have done if you'd been the one to go down into the Murk and get the box?"

He thought for a moment. "Probably left it down there," he said. "Literally bring him back a couple of quarters, then come back later myself and get it. Bring it to a pawn shop if it didn't have a gold bar in it." He paused again. "Or just bust it over the head of the monster, maybe, if I thought I could get away with it."

"Right," I said. "Julie. What about you?"

I could tell that Julie was getting where I was going with this. She sighed. "I would have given the whole thing to him, unopened," she said. "I wouldn't even have *wanted* to open it."

I nodded. "So it's official," I said. "We're not the 'Fear Club.' We're the goddamned *Fool* Club! We're just a bunch of fucking *tools* that Mike Flowers knows exactly how to use."

Steve, miraculously, didn't laugh. He stalked over to the small window at the back of the room that looked out onto the grove of ash trees surrounding the property, dark grey in the drizzling morning light.

Julie touched the box gingerly. "But he didn't get away with *everything*," she said.

I closed my eyes and leaned my head back against the wall. "How do you mean?" I asked.

"Magic," she said. "It's *real*. Monsters! All fucking *real*. We *know* that!"

"Do we, though?" I said. "Where are we right now? We were all in the same wing of the hospital the night that Mike died—what do you remember after that?"

Golem Creek General Hospital was small, so far as city hospitals go, but fully outfitted and functional. I was there for pneumonia, and half out of my wits. Steve was in the next room over, recovering from one of his usual exploits: he had ridden a dirt bike quite literally off a small cliff, and had casts on one leg and one arm. Julie was there visiting Steve, and sat reading quietly beside his bed while his pain meds kicked in. Michael Flowers was fitted out in one of the larger rooms located directly across the hall.

He was dying. He had been admitted earlier that night, in critical condition. A deep stab wound had punctured several abdominal organs. After hours of surgery, his system had gone septic, and he had been carted to that room, just across the hall, comatose. Where was his family? They were getting ready to pull the plug. But he was alone at that moment.

"You *remember*, don't you?" I said. "That weird

purple light, radiating out of Mike's room and into ours? And suddenly I'm perfectly okay. Steve, you got up out of bed, insisting that Julie help you, and the only reason you couldn't walk perfectly was because of the *cast* on your leg. Nothing broken. We all walked out into the hallway. We all walked into Mike's room—"

"And then we woke up the next morning," Julie said. "Steve was already arguing with the doctors when I woke up on that little couch in his room."

"That *light*," Steve said, turning around. "It was like he *was* that light. Remember? He was just dissolving into it. A cloud of purple light."

"Guys," I said. "What if everything we saw last night *didn't even happen?*"

The usual exuberant dismissal from Steve was not forthcoming. Miracles upon miracles.

"One way to find out," Julie said. "We've got to go. Back to Amanda's. Back to the Murk." She got up and brushed herself off. "Stupid box," she said, gazing down at it.

"No shit," Steve said, striding over to it. "Stupid little fucking box."

He kicked it. The room exploded.

part two

∽

THE MURK

L OCATION: CJ's, A BAR way out in Bum-
fuck, Egypt (i.e., past Jenks). Discovered
while trying to overcome boredom. Staley said he
wanted to actually do something the other night
that didn't involve comic books or weed. We took the
red jeep, since the previous night had the Pontiac
nearly fucked. First flight of hell-hounds? Piece of
piss. Although narrowly missed getting our asses
chewed by those sonsabitches.

So Booker has to take a piss—this is at CJ's—
and he's so fucking wasted he somehow wanders
into the owner's office and out a back door. He sees
something going on out there—some dude dressed
all in black, and another guy, and he thinks it's
probably a drug deal or some weirdo sex thing he
doesn't want to get involved in, so he turns tail and
runs. But he runs the wrong *fucking way!*

We're cracking up at this point, when he's
telling us this. He says he still needs to take a
piss, but now he's out in the fucking woods and
he's all turned around. So he whips it out and takes

*a piss, and while he's doing that, his eyes adjust
to the darkness, and he sees something out there,
a little farther out in the woods.*

*Booker's got no fucking sense, so he just wan-
ders out there, and whaddaya know? It's ruins, basically. Looks like a house that burned down. And
he's like: "Is this that fucking Devil House? Oh,
man!" He finds what looks like a chimney and a
few of the remaining wall supports. He can't barely
see much of anything, so he finally tries to find his
way back to CJ's.*

Somehow, he walks in the front *door of CJ's,
and the rest of us look up and we're like, "Where
the fuck you been?" He orders another beer, the
dumb bastard, and he tells us his story.*

*So we pay up and we tip that hot-ass waitress
probably fifty percent. Then we head out to the car
and wait for the assholes outside the bar to shut
up and go home. Then we all follow Booker's lead
out back, but this time we've got flashlights and
rope and combat knives, and we make sure Fitz has
the camera. Because, basically, we're figuring that
we're going to run into some shit back there, you
know?*

*It takes us about ten minutes to find the place
and another fifteen before I nearly break my leg
falling through an overgrown hole in the floor.
Booker drags me back out, and we're shining our
flashlights down there—there's all sorts of shit
down there, but it looks like someone locked up
a fucking gorilla in a hotel room. Staley's already
rigging up one of the ropes to some steel dowel rods,
and Fitz gets the video camera recording.*

*Once we're all down there, we figure this must
be the old Murdock House, because it's even got the
magic circle still on the ground, and still smells
like something burned. So I guess that question's
answered, at least. But there's no skeleton, or anything, so either we weren't the first to come down
here after it happened or Murdock somehow escaped without the Devil getting him. At least not
that night.*

*And Staley's like: "Dudes! Check this shit out!"
Because there's a sort of false door, and I don't
know how the hell he found it, but back behind this
one part of the wall we find a little room, also kind
of fucked up. And that's where the portal was—*

PETE JARRY RUBBED HIS eyes. It was about one-
thirty in the afternoon, by the clock, but down here
in the den you couldn't tell time worth shit. He'd
gotten up maybe half an hour ago, and the first
thing he did, after starting the coffee, was drag all
that stuff out of the closet and spread it out in
front of him.

He was reading the spiral-bound notebook,
starting from the beginning.

He started skimming the contents, page by
page. They had a numbering system that looked
like some kind of date, but he couldn't be sure.
160696.2302: Sketch of portal. 230696.0011: Map of
one relevant area of "Tulsa" (not to scale). 230696.
Supp.: Second encounter with the "hell-hounds."

Many pages later (221196.2202):

Totally stuffed! Smoked a joint with Pete to-

night. Everything cool until we tried to find some-
thing to listen to. Staley alternately happy and
sad. The Sex Pistols. Happy. The Bee-Gees? Sad.
Booker being a jackass puts on "Stayin' Alive" and
Pete goes into some sort of weird trance.

Pete stopped reading for a moment. Did he remember that?

Anyway, we ended up leaving because none of
us could get him out of it. At least we managed to
score a decent dinner before the big hunt.
231196.0311: Complete waste of fucking time
when it came to the hunt. One good thing came out
of it, though: when we got back to Pete's, Stek was
there and we had a chance to talk to him again. Got
the Lovecraft book from him, Bloodcurdling Tales.
He said: "Look more closely at the underlined parts.
And check out the inside back cover." So when
we got back to Booker's mom's house, Staley and
Booker started on it.
Too bad there's no turkey here, I'm fucking
starving.

This was followed by what appeared to be a grocery
list of some sort—*tortilla chips, queso, PIZZA, QT*
hot dogs, BEER, etc. The next page had a dark
stain on it, with a sketch of something labeled
"phaser gun" and a big X scrawled through most of
it.

Then, occupying the center of an otherwise
blank page, Pete saw this:

SUIQT OLAHQ.
(Just a reminder.)

jfaetbi cilwboq
ylu juqs aus lus efq ebtos!

SETKHQ QSBH!!!

PETE SAT BACK, SOMEWHAT baffled and amused. "Oh, *right!*" he said aloud. "Where is that secret decoder thing?" Laughing, he got up and headed for his stash in the Easter Island head on the altar.

STEVE ROLLED ANOTHER NATURAL twenty. "Direct hit!" he said. "*Bam!*"

This I awoke to: Steve's voice, as obnoxious and presumptuous as always, muffled by intervening walls, coming from somewhere nearby.

I opened my eyes. The prismatic light of a crisp, spring morning peeked through a panoramic window at one end of the room. I lay in a bed—a king-size, *hotel* bed.

I sat up.

"Ouch!" a different voice exclaimed joyously. Someone clapped their hands. "*That* guy's toast!"

On one wall: a stylized map of what appeared to be a college campus, framed in wood and drawn in three-dimensional perspective. The invigorating aroma of coffee in a percolator on a wooden desk alerted me to the scent of eggs and bacon, frying merrily somewhere outside the room.

I swung my legs out of the bed and noticed that I was wearing flannel pajamas. My jeans and T-shirt, hooded jacket and underclothes, lay neatly folded and apparently clean on another little table.

I could stand. Very easily. I was not—*dead*, was I?

Voices, one of them obviously Steve's, still murmured somewhere outside of the hotel room.

I got up and strode over to the window, at which point I practically fell over. Once again I questioned my relative degree of corporeality.

Outside the window, some distance away, like the sight of mountains from a valley, stood a pyramid of such vast and incredible majesty, I could barely comprehend it. I rubbed my eyes. I gazed out the window again.

Still there.

The window appeared to be a few stories above an empty parking lot, which backed up to a run of little hills with a highway behind them. There were trees, forests of them actually, and buildings— houses, shops, convenience stores...a fucking *strip mall...?*

Curiously, though, the place seemed—well, *empty.* No cars moving on the road, no people strolling about. Nothing.

I changed into the clean clothes and poured myself a cup of coffee. After one tentative sip, I had to avoid burning myself in an attempt to chug the entire thing. I poured myself another.

In the bathroom, I found hairbrush, toothbrush, mouthwash—everything. After ensuring that I looked once more the part of Charles Leland, Captain of Whatever, I proceeded boldly out of the room.

WITH A DRAMATIC FLOURISH, the little man—who looked like an emeritus professor of philosophy from some quaint liberal arts college—scribbled on a sheet of scratch paper. "As the creature expires before you," he pronounced, "it rolls to the side, revealing a door set into the wall of the cavern." His warbly voice reminded me of an excited cartoon character.

Steve's eyes widened. "I approach the door," he said.

The hall outside my room opened onto a large meeting area a few doors down. By the look of the maps, dice, and pewter figurines strewn about on one of the tables, Steve and the "professor" were in the midst of playing Dungeons & Dragons.

The little man continued. "The shimmering of gold pieces heaped about the room momentarily blinds you—"

"Charley!" Steve noticed my approach. He began waving excitedly. "This guy is the single *best* DM in the *entire fucking universe*!"

The little man responded with the most genuine smile I had ever seen, unblemished by even a hint of self-consciousness. "That's so *very* kind of you!" he said. "It's a passion of mine!" He adjusted his wire-rimmed spectacles. "Tea? Coffee?" he inquired, lifting his eyebrows at me. "Or something else? I've probably got it!" He chuckled, indicating a few plates sitting on an empty table nearby, bearing the remains of breakfast.

I lifted the half-empty Styrofoam cup I had with me. "I'm good, thanks," I said, trying to sound normal. "Um—"

"Julie's downstairs," Steve said, idly shaking a handful of dice. "She's *reading*," he said with mock disdain.

I nodded. "Great, uh—" I wasn't quite sure how to respond to any of this. I decided to simply dive in. "Steve?"

Steve was making an annotation on his player character sheet as the "DM" adjusted a few figurines on a grid between them. "Yeah?" he responded, not looking up.

"Um—where the *fuck* are we?" I blurted out.

Steve laughed. The little old man looked up at me, pursing his lips as if to keep from joining in Steve's response, then bowed his head gracefully and stood up.

"I," he said, striding over to me and reaching out one pale, thin hand in greeting, "am the Dreamkeeper."

I shook his hand limply. "Okay?" I said.

He patted a little, immaculate badge pinned onto his light-green cardigan sweater. "You can call me Roland." The name was etched neatly on its faux brass background. "PROP." it read beneath it. I immediately got the feeling that the name "Roland" was merely a convenience.

"Good to meet you, uh, Roland," I said, feeling lame and a little embarrassed.

He nodded, smiling, not missing a beat. "And this," he continued, waving his hand about him, "is my Emporium!"

I gazed about the room. It was cool—kind of. There was an old-school cigarette machine on one wall, next to a jukebox. Booths and tables and chairs. Two racks against another wall, one filled with magazines and the other stuffed with paperbacks. A comic book spinner display. Something that looked like a checkout counter fronted the area, with an old cash register set on top of glass display cases, beyond which was a little entrance-way: a sort of "front door" with a glass window in it, through which I could see only darkness.

I forced a smile. "Wow," I said dryly.

The Dreamkeeper smiled even more widely. "Oh, Charles, I apologize!" he began. His warbling, cartoonish tone was strangely endearing. "I really, *really* do! Your friends awoke some time ago—we simply didn't want to disturb you. They insisted that I let you get some much-needed *sleep!*"

I nodded. "Thanks?" I said.

"I think—oh, I don't know," the Dreamkeeper turned to Steve, who was flipping through one of the rule manuals stacked next to him. "What do you think, Steve?"

Steve looked up. "Oh, *man*, Charley!" he exclaimed. "When I tell you that you *ain't ready for this*, you gotta *believe* that you *ain't* ready for this shit, my man!"

"I ENCOURAGE YOU TO wander—truly *wander*— with the utmost disrespect of convention or intentionality," the Dreamkeeper said. He paused momentarily, his eyes searching some invisible space above and beyond me. "Boy, doesn't that just *ruin*

it? How can you *find out* what you're looking for
if you're looking for some *thing* before you start?"
He seemed genuinely baffled by this question.

"At any rate," he continued, waving his hand
toward the entranceway. "Have at it!"

"*Wait* a second," I said, trying to resist the
Dreamkeeper's infectious enthusiasm. "I get what
you're saying. Thank you for the invitation. Thank
you for the hospitality. But I don't think either of
you are quite answering my real question here—"

"Charley! Charley," Steve got up reluctantly
from his seat. He strode over to me and clamped
a firm hand on my shoulder. "Just *trust me* for a
second, okay?"

"Ex*cuse* me, Steve?" I said. "*Trust* you? Forgive
me if I'm out of *practice* on that count—"

Steve was chuckling again. "I would go with
you," he said, patting me on the shoulder and
heading back to his seat, "but it just wouldn't have
the same degree of explanatory *power*. You dig?"

Roland the Dreamkeeper had stepped back a
pace. His smile continued unabated.

I took a deep breath. "Okay," I said, heading toward the entrance. "Fine." Something about
Steve's unhesitating confidence in the situation,
combined with Roland the Dreamkeeper's utter
lack of affectation despite the context of what he
was saying, made the decision for me. I turned to
face the entranceway.

"Oh, wait," Roland said, reaching into his shirt
pocket. "You should take this."

He handed me a plain old Bic ballpoint pen—
the kind you can buy in packs of twenty for a

dollar—and immediately headed back to the game table.

"Thanks?" I said, and stood there dumbly for a moment holding it out in front of me, waiting for some sort of explanation. The only thing unusual about it was some writing on one side of the cap, done in the same white stenciling as the words on the pen's body. It read "Box 1132."

Roland had returned to the game. "That's a hell of a lot of XP there," he said, rubbing his hands together eagerly. "Now, you realize that without the Sword of Astonishment, you still don't have much of a chance against the Silent Goblin Gang outside—"

"Where's Julie again?" I asked.

"Somewhere downstairs," Steve said.

I walked briskly to the door. Gazing through it up close, I *could*, in fact, see what appeared to be a stock room, piled high with boxes on shelves from floor to ceiling, and lit by fluorescent track lighting.

"Yay, Charley-boy!" Steve cheered behind me mockingly. I turned to see him pumping both fists into the air. "Go for it! Show 'em how it's done!" I shook my head. His laughter followed me through the door, into what I "couldn't possibly be ready for."

AND I DEFINITELY WAS *not*.

All the world could not have prepared me for the Dreamkeeper's Emporium. Not midnight resurrections, not sorcerous boxes with spellbooks and magical keys, not bat-winged demons nor horned half-wolf humanoids—*nothing.*

The cavernous, winding labyrinth of the Emporium stretched out in seemingly endless array from my point of departure. I tried to make a mental note amidst the sheer jam-packedness of *cool stuff* and fantastic distractions in the place of where I had left Steve and Roland.

The hall I initially found myself traversing continued endlessly—and I found no evidence that this could be just a figure of speech. Both sides of the hall were decked in movie posters and artwork of the most extraordinary variety, between numerous doors, no one of which seemed quite the same in appearance as any of the others.

I made a sincere effort to form a more general mental layout, but the place got the better of me in short order. The only thing that seemed reasonably consistent were openings into sitting areas around decorative water fountains that appeared every now and then. Beside these you could find immaculate restrooms, what appeared to be slots in the wall for mail next to sets of PO boxes, and knick-knack shops that "sold" refreshments, souvenirs for all sorts of random locations (I thought the "Wish You Were *Here*?" shot glasses, with little pictures of the Empire State building or the Eiffel Tower amusing), along with a wide variety of stationery, envelopes, stamps, and, surprisingly, lottery tickets. After the sixth or seventh turn down the eighth or ninth hallway, I stopped trying to keep track. The sheer *volume* of *stuff* was overpowering and incredible.

I began to try doors at random. A number of

them opened onto strangely prosaic displays that resembled little hotel or motel rooms, such as the one I had awoken in, but with windows looking out on various types of intricate outdoor scenery. One room had a window looking out onto piles of new-fallen snow; upon opening the window, a freezing cold blast of air flooded the room, which kicked the room's wall-unit heater on. I waved my hand about outside the window. Cold. *Real*—or so it felt. The room "next door" to it had a window looking out onto a crisp spring morning dawning over a sea of oak trees, the scent of fresh blooming flowers floating on a light breeze.

Other doors opened onto rooms piled high with stacks of old, crumbling newspapers...window furnishings displayed on various types of frames...old clothes strewn about art-deco furniture, smelling like mothballs...boxes with odd labels handwritten in marker on them (my favorite read: "This is a box of pizza boxes. The pizza has been eaten!"). One room even opened into a small foyer with another, identical door at the end of it, which opened *back* into the hallway I had come from (I went back and forth in both directions twice just to make sure).

I must have spent *hours* just basking in the radiant weirdness of it all. Rooms upon rooms. And as I progressed through it, it changed and grew, almost as if it was somehow *learning* about me from my reactions. A perfect replica of a comic book store from my youth—Fantasy Comics (even the comics hadn't changed!). A music studio, drums and bass and guitar and microphones all set up and ready to go on the other side of the sound-room glass. The concessions area of a movie theater, which let out into another set of hallways leading to *full-size movie theaters*, a few of which were playing films—almost as if they were bored of not being used. Fifteen minutes of the original *Back to the Future* convinced me that the entire movie would be played, perfectly, from beginning to end, were I to stay and watch it.

The place *did* seem to be missing one crucial element, however.

People.

There were none. Zero. Not a soul graced the halls or rooms—although their handiwork appeared in every way, shape, and form no matter where you looked.

That is, until I stumbled upon Julie.

THE SMOKING ROOM—FOR so the plaque above the door read in exquisite calligraphy—was a little nook outfitted with a grand, old armchair beset on one side with a fat, intricately carved tobacco pipe; on the other side of the armchair was a pleasantly hooded reading lamp and a stack of what appeared to be old '80s paperbacks. Seated comfortably in its midst, sheer joy enveloping her features, was Julie Evergreen

"Julie?" I said quietly.

She gazed up at me. "Charles!" she spoke kind of slowly, as if my name was a lovely memory she was unwilling to let go of. "I haven't read these since—" Julie's voice caught for a moment. "I had to sit down for a bit."

The warm little room had a small, cozy fire

crackling in a fireplace and walls covered floor to ceiling with neatly framed pictures and drawings and portraits—most appeared to be of scenes from classic fantasy novels like *Alice in Wonderland.* I happened to notice a weird-looking version of the caterpillar scene, with the caterpillar sitting on what looked like a bean bag chair instead of a mushroom.

I nodded. "I was just—" I started.

Julie busied herself lighting the pipe with a long match from the side-table. She took a few puffs. "Meerschaum," she said. "And this is" — she paused, frowning, and then smiling— "*periqué.* Soaked in...rum!"

I nodded again. "Right," I said. I was unsure of how to continue—not to mention the fact that she seemed so genuinely...well, *happy.* I had never witnessed *this* Julie Evergreen.

She smiled up at me, folding the book in her lap. "Have a seat!" she insisted, waving at a little couch shoved between two bookshelves.

I obliged her and sat. Above me, a detailed oil painting of a wise old cat, crouched in the midst of more books and a yellow table-clock, gazed in earnest down at me.

"So," I began, trying to choose my words with care. "About this Dreamkeeper place—"

"I am happier than I've ever been," Julie said to me, her smile broadening. "In my entire life."

"That's—" I interrupted myself again. How was I supposed to respond to *that*? I decided to cut out all the bullshit—happy Julie or no. "Julie, *what the fuck is going on?*"

The smile didn't diminish. "I think," she responded, "that we may be *dead*, Charley."

I sighed. Dead? Okay, maybe. But I had a suspicion that it wasn't so. A nagging hunch.

"All right," I said. "All right! All right." I leaned forward. "But what about Mike Flowers? *He* was dead *too*. That didn't seem to make much of a difference."

Julie seemed undeterred. "Nevertheless," she said.

"'Nevertheless,'" I quoted. "Are you *kidding* me? Look, I woke up today and saw a goddamned *pyramid* outside my window. A *pyramid*! Do you understand me? Steve kicked that box and *something* happened—"

"It blew up," she said. "We died. Case closed. Just accept it, Charley."

"Did you *see* the fucking pyramid?" I asked. "Because I'd consider that pretty fucking out of the ordinary, Julie."

"Yes, I saw it," she said. "Steve saw it too. And yes it's out of the ordinary. So what?"

"So *what*?" I responded. "So you can't just *assume* that you're *dead* now! And even if you did— hey, did you ever think that maybe weirdness like that should be *investigated*?"

Julie was shaking her head. "No," she said. "Not always."

I was getting a little concerned. "Hey, Julie, come *on*," I pleaded. "I need somebody else to help me, here. You and I both know that Steve's not going to listen to reason. But *you*—"

"What if I *want* to be dead, Charley?" she said.

I stopped myself.

"Don't you understand?" she continued. "That *other* fucking life? The one where I'm always fucking trying to get *out* of doing stuff?" She laughed bitterly. "Oh, yeah, great, *another* day of fucking school. Another day where I'm either guilty because I *didn't* do something or guilty because I *did*?"

I could sense the memory of her Ordeal swimming just below the surface of her outburst. "I'm constantly figuring out how to check out early, Charley. Even just a *little bit*." She sighed and set the book down on the table beside her. "My only two friends are a fucking *psychopath* and *you*," she said, turning to look at me. "And I am sick and tired of being your *goddamned chauffeur*."

Julie opened a little drawer beside her and pulled out a long, black cigarette. Thick smoke billowed out of her mouth after she lit it, along with the scent of burning cloves.

I felt instantly sorry I had tried to push her. "Julie, hey," I said. I stood up. "I'm sorry."

She sighed. "I know," she said. "I know. Me, too."

"Julie," I continued, "you know what? You're right." I reached for the cigarette. She handed it to me and I took a long, deep drag. Clove X-Tras. It figured that you had to fucking die and go to heaven in order to come across them ever again.

"You're right," I repeated. "So what if we don't ever have to deal with Mike Flowers again?"

As I said it, the truth of the statement became abundantly clear to me. I handed back the cigarette.

"It was *our* choice to keep dealing with him," I said. "It was *always* our choice! We never *had* to do anything."

Julie gazed at me. "I just need a break, Charley," she said. "There's nothing back there that I want to return to. You said it yourself, remember? 'No more school, no more books.'"

I recalled our conversation—had that really only been a few days ago?

"A break," I said. "I understand." I turned to go.

"Charley?" she said.

I paused. "What?" I responded.

"Are you just going to *go*?" she asked.

"Yes," I said. "You're right. You need a break." I stepped outside the entrance to the Smoking Room. "But this is just too fucking weird. It's cool—it's *awesome*, actually. But *I've got to know what's going on*."

She nodded.

"I'll—be back, I guess?" I said.

I started down the hallway, back in the direction I *thought* would lead me to the entrance of the Emporium.

IT FELT LIKE MANY hours before I came upon something I truly didn't expect.

EXIT. The little metal sign with glowing red letters was visible at the far end of a large vestibule dedicated entirely to Christmas decorations opening up at the conclusion of one hallway. The Christmas vestibule reminded me of a department store

during the holiday season, with high-ceilinged arch-
ways lined in multicolored lights and ornamental
pine cones. A clean, reflective, fake-stone floor surrounded glass cases filled with perfumes and jewelry.
I could even smell some of the high-priced perfumes
from testers sitting on the counter.

There it was, though. EXIT. A blank metal
door with one of those lockable push-bars on it
rested innocently beneath it. *Who, me?*

When I approached the door, I noticed that
there was a lectern set up beside it with something
that looked like a guest book on it, lying open. Half-
incomprehensible signatures adorned part of each
two-column page, and beside the signature, more
clearly printed (I noticed upon inspection that the
second column said above it, in fine print, "ᴘʟᴇᴀѕᴇ
ᴘʀɪɴᴛ ᴄʟᴇᴀʀʟʏ"), what looked to be *place names.*

Only a few of them appeared to be in roman
characters that I could read. The rest rose and
fell from the page in all sorts of wild scribbles
and loops and ligatures, some resembling alpha-
bets I recognized but could not read, such as Man-
darin and Greek. Of the ones in an alphabet that
I could read appeared a number I knew of among
others of which I had never heard. "Plainfield"
and "Seattle" and "Manhattan"..."Providence" and
"Vancouver"..."Sunnydale" and "Arkham" and "Hill
Valley"..."*Golem Creek*" and "*Tulsa*"...

Gingerly, I tried to push open the door. It
wouldn't budge.

Suspecting the obvious, I looked back at the
"guest book."

"ᴘʟᴇᴀѕᴇ ᴘʀɪɴᴛ ᴄʟᴇᴀʀʟʏ" gazed back at me.

I looked around for a pen, and suddenly remembered the Bic pen that Roland the Dreamkeeper had given me.

"What the hell?" I said aloud. The temptation to find out whether it worked or not seized me utterly. I could just write the words, sign it, and simply peek through the door. If it worked, then Steve and Julie and I had a way out of this place, assuming things turned sour.

If it didn't... I had a pretty strong suspicion that the damned thing was going to work. I signed my name with a flourish, and wrote "Golem Creek" as clearly as I could beside it. An audible click sounded from the door, which I immediately opened and peered through.

Awoke this morning in something of a daze, Charles wrote in his journal that evening. *What have I done? The meeting with the Witch... What have I DONE? The Creature must have been a product of that spell...and now Molly, my precious Molly Furnival—*

He stopped, tapping the page with his pen. The little journal was a bit small, but it was the only thing the nurse could find down in the gift shop. Kind of her to get it for him. The dim lights of his hospital room seemed to flicker a bit, but he was feeling lucid enough to try and write down at least *something* of what he recalled. Perhaps writing it out the way it all happened would make it more...objective, somehow? He could hardly bear it any longer: the sense of *confusion* that seemed to lie just beneath every thought, word, and action. It certainly wasn't the booze; he had been sober for almost a week now. Certainly the pneumonia had something to do with it...but the confusion still lay there beneath the surface, somehow *more* than just the illness, obscuring something, a memory, a *meaning* he was missing...like a dream that you *knew* you had, but you *just couldn't bring back...*

Perhaps he could start with the night that the Creature—that slavering beast, like a man and beast hybrid—had stolen Molly from him. Then back up a bit, get a grip on the consequences of his actions.

Dear, sweet Molly. Couldn't she see that he was trying to *save* her from that drug-addled maniac she seemed so absurdly fond of? And he *did* love her, and felt reasonably sure that she also loved him...but what *foolishness* had he allowed to take her from him?

Carefully, he tore out the page on which he had just written. He tried again.

27 Dec., he wrote. Was that horrible night *really* only a week ago? *Broken-hearted, banished to this strange tavern in a weird corner of this world...*

Much better. Curwen's Witch had made it quite clear that for every blessing, there would be an equivalent curse. Those blasted rules. What was the point of *real magic* if you weren't actually *getting away* with anything?

Charles wrote it all down, starting with that terrible night. He got out the sheet of paper upon which he had later recorded the strange message in code at the end of the hall, still tucked carefully into a copy of Dostoevsky's *The Idiot*—they were supposed to be discussing it in Howland's class after winter break. He still had *no idea* what the message implied or entailed. Nonetheless, he dutifully copied it into the context of his "confession."

There had been no *clues* anywhere to be found, that next day. He had awoken, aching head as usual, back in his apartment, still soaking wet from traversing the rains the night before. He had a sinking feeling that the headache and nausea he felt was more than a simple hangover—as indeed turned out to be the case. But he returned despite this—*he had to know if he had really seen her...*

It took some time to find the door labeled "TRAP." Ha, ha. At the end of the hall? The plaque with the message, unmolested, still incomprehensible. Behind the frosted-glass door...?

Nothing. Or, rather, no signs of a party or of any sort of gathering whatsoever. A storage room for extra chairs. Some racks for coats. The door left unlocked, even, almost as an apology for its lack of available *clues*.

He could practically hear the Witch laughing at him. What was it she had said to him that day, when he had finally had enough of the pain, the loneliness, being without Molly, imagining her in the hands of that awful, blasted *décadent*, of all things?

"For these fools of men and their woes, care not thou at all."

That was it. A warning. But she had given him the formula from that old book anyway—perhaps to watch him squirm, to make him understand, to convince him, ultimately, that it was *Curwen's* power he was playing with. A simple, grade-school test for the know-it-all, whose time had come.

In recounting the circumstances regarding Curwen's Witch, Charles was careful to clearly delineate the issue.

Friends with an old Faery Queen, or so she claimed— although she laughed as she said it. Practically impossible to thoroughly understand; she didn't just speak in riddles, but in conversation with invisible people in the same room with you. And I should have known that after my interaction with her, after the working of the spell—so simple, it turned out— nothing would be the same.

The first night, I slept soundly, except for dreams that seemed to repeat my encounter with her, over and over again. When I awoke, the room seemed...different, somehow, changed. Not quite the right room anymore. And this feeling continued, becoming more extraordinary. I would begin to think of something, a food I craved, a book I longed to read, a person I hadn't seen in ages, and within moments, something would happen that resulted in my encounter with that thing or person.

The initial pleasantness of this experience gave way to an underlying anxiety, for occasionally things I did not want to experience would also occur; a fall, a loss, any of a myriad of problems. The clock read one-thirty or ten-twenty or whatever...but sleeping—or, rather, dreaming—seemed to have overtaken waking, so what did it matter? The world seemed now to be merely playing dice with me, manifesting desires and fears at random...but where had the objective world gone, the one I so hated and feared before?

There is another world, and the magic it contains sometimes bleeds out into this one. Sometimes we can "cut it" in just the right way that it bleeds when we want it to. I feel it is necessary to explain, you see, that I seemed to have stumbled upon a key to the whole mystery. A solution. A means of escape from my own terrible fallibility. And I fear to put it in writing...I fear it...but it must be said: there was a thing I loved more than Molly Furnival, and it was the power to make her love me... The Witch, it seemed, had been right: "For these fools of men and their woes, care not thou at all." I had been a fool, a common man, and I had paid as a fool always does. "But there is that which remains."

Something shook Charles as he wrote the words. *Key...means of escape...* What was it about a key?

He began to feel his fever returning in full force. He flipped back through the pages. It almost appalled him that the weight of the pages of his confession seemed somehow lighter now than the weight of his guilt. The little square of letters. There it was. *Dobbsfkdq, Aetoibq!...* But how in the world was he supposed to...?

The door said "TRAP." It was a trap-door; funny, clever...a clue?

It was the only other anomaly he could think of. But how to make use of it?

There *was* something he recalled...

Oh, gods, it CAN'T be that simple!

At that moment, a strange mist, scintillating with a purplish-mauve light, came flooding into his hospital room. Almost without meaning to, Charles let the pen fall into the folds of the sheets, and set the little journal on the table by the bed. He swung his legs over the edge of the bed and took a few tentative steps on the cold floor.

His head was...*clear.*

He followed the pulsings of light out of his room.

"AND HE FALLS TO his *death*, off Juggler's Ledge, into the Pit of Demented Pixies."

Roland the Dreamkeeper grinned as he spoke, then simultaneously lifted his tea cup and bowed his head slightly.

Steve's eyes were enormous. He dropped his pencil, a broad smile replacing his astonishment, and began slowly to clap his hands together dramatically. "Bravo," he breathed, beginning to clap more furiously. "*Bravo!*" He yelled it out, then stood and whooped dramatically, striding about the room.

"I can't *believe* it!" he said, still standing, practically shaking with excitement. "That's—that was absolutely—I can't *believe* it!"

Roland simply sat and grinned, sipping his tea, absorbing the praise impersonally, like a collection plate absorbs sin. "It's been a *long* time since I've had a truly *excellent* player character, Steve!" he said. "By all means, it is important that you pat yourself on the back. Without your interest and excitement, the words are just marks on a page or vibrations in the air—they mean nothing."

Steve still hummed with excitement. He glanced over the large wooden table before them, now strewn mercilessly with maps and dice, scraps of paper bearing numerous notes and calculations, precisely sculpted miniatures that truly seemed to *come alive* as they played—especially his own, the

hero, the half-elf thief Graxx, magically enhanced
dexterity and all. The remains of a truly exquisite
"lunch" of potato chips and cheeseburgers, washed
down with freezing Jolt cola (which Steve felt *certain* they had stopped making a decade ago), sat
on TV-tray tables to the side. Steve could still
scent the delicious frying grease from the little
miraculous diner down one of the halls, where he
and Roland had briefly gone, ostensibly to recoup,
but really just to delay the end of the game. Full,
freshly cooked meals had already been laid out for
them there, though no cook was in sight.

"But you played the *rest of the party*," Steve
said, admiration infusing his voice. "All *seven other
characters in my party*, without ever *once* getting
tripped up! Not *ever*! How—?"

"As I said," Roland replied, "it's a passion of
mine."

Steve found it impossible not to continue smiling. His dream come true. The greatest D & D
adventure imaginable.

"Not to mention," Roland added, leaning back
in his chair, "that game's only one of my lesser
accomplishments. You should see some of my actual
full-blown *campaigns*!"

Steve collapsed to the floor upon hearing this,
only partially for dramatic effect.

Julie walked into the room, smiling broadly. An
aroma of fine tobacco wafted in with her. "Hey!"
she said. Cheerful, relaxed—what creature was
this? Certainly not Julie Evergreen... "What's up?"

Steve raised himself back into his seat. "What's
up? Oh, Jules, this is just incredible—"

"Tell me about it!" Julie said, reclining into one of the chairs. "Roland, did you know that you had the entire *Monster Sitter* series back there? I thought there were only *four*... I've been reading those for *hours* now—there's got to be sixty or seventy of them—"

"Certainly!" Roland said. "And those stories just keep getting *more intricate*, don't they?"

Julie nodded. "Where on earth did you *find* them?"

Roland chuckled. "Here and there," he said. "And. You know!"

"Where's Charley?" Steve asked.

Julie blinked. "Oh, right," she said. "I'm not sure. He wandered off."

"Wandered off?" Steve repeated.

Roland did his usual chuckle as he stood up. "Your friend Charley is exactly where he needs to be, right now. Don't you realize? We're all exactly where we need to be, every *time*," he said, the peculiar emphasis on the word "time" noticeable. He started off toward one of the back hallways.

"Hey, wait!" Steve shouted, standing up. "What about—"

"Calm down, Steve, my friend!" Roland said, his voice fading. "Just got to do a little inventory, that's all. No cause for alarm."

Julie gazed after him as he retreated a few paces, then disappeared around a corner. "Right where we need to be?" she said.

Steve shrugged, sitting back down. "I have no idea what the fuck that means," he said. "But I can tell you one thing: I ain't going *anywhere*! This place fucking rocks. Did you know that there's a fucking *movie theater* somewhere in here? Roland told me. He said he's been collecting movies forever. Probably got damn-near everything by now. I was going to try and find it later, maybe see if I could watch *Die Hard* again! Can you imagine that? Fucking *movie theater*—fucking *Die Hard*! *In* the movie theater!"

Julie sat down. "Yeah," she said, sounding troubled.

"Are you hungry?" he asked. "There's a little diner back there, too. We can go get a burger. I think."

"I'm—" Julie paused, trying to formulate the right words. The conversation with Charley had finally started getting to her. "Worried?"

Steve responded with an automatic grimace. "You should be *ashamed* of yourself, little girl!" he said, wagging a finger at her dramatically. He began doing a poor imitation of Marlon Brando in *The Godfather*. "All this I do for you? And this is how you *repay* me?"

Julie allowed a half-smile. "I'm just—I mean— *what the hell do we do* now*?*"

Steve seemed genuinely taken aback. "What do you *mean*?" he said. "What do we do *now*? Whatever we damn well please!" He leaned back in his chair and extracted a few Twizzlers from a package beside him. "This is just *typical*, you know? We finally get to it—we finally make it to fucking Never-Never Land—and you read a few books and you're *done*? What do you want? You want to go back *there*?" He jerked his thumb behind him and bit off half of a Twizzler. "Because, you know," he said, chewing, "I mean, that's the way. I guess. Just go back. Go to that pyramid and, I guess, I don't know, lie down in it? Is that how you get back?"

"That's what's *bothering* me, Steve!" Julie said. "I *don't* know how to get back! Is this really such a great place if we don't have a way out of it?"

"Ask Roland!" Steve responded. "Ask Roland, if you're so interested. He'll fucking know. That guy knows everything!"

"Okay, I will," Julie stood up, turning back toward the hallways. "I'll ask him. I'll find out."

Steve sighed. "Look, Julie, I'm sorry," he said. "I just don't get it. I really don't agree with you. I think we should just chill here for as long as we goddamned *can*, you know? What do they say? 'Don't look a gift horse in the mouth.'" He paused. "Why do they say that again?"

Julie was shifting her glance from one side to the other. "You saw where he went, didn't you?"

"No, I didn't," Steve said. He took a bite out of another Twizzler.

Julie approached the main hall that started back from the "checkout counter," then retreated again. "Oh, crap," she said. "I have no fucking idea where he went."

"So go look around," Steve said. He got up and headed over to an old cigarette machine that sat in one corner, next to a jukebox. "I'll wait here. And tell you what? I'm such a good friend, that when Roland gets back, if you haven't found him, I'll ask him where the exit is myself." He grabbed a quarter from a stack that sat on top of the cigarette machine, waved it at Julie, and dropped it into the slot. "Love this place," he said, smiling. He pulled a handle, and a pack of Camel nonfilters ka-chucked into the receptacle at the bottom of the machine.

Julie took a few steps down one hall. "Not this one?" she said. Softly playing guitar music came from the room behind her.

"This one's for you, Jules!" Steve said. "'Member this? Santo & Johnny. 'Sleepwalk.'"

Julie returned to the main room. "I'm going to try a different approach," she said, and walked over to a curtained wall at the other end of the room. Steve was now reclining in a little booth by the wall, flipping nonchalantly through what appeared to be a copy of *Detective Comics* #27, oblivious.

She drew the curtain aside. A glass shop-front door stood behind it, through which she could see a small, brightly lit parking lot, empty of vehicles. A pitch-black night sky, ornamented with a calm, full moon, obscured the reaches beyond, just past a verge lined with pine trees.

When she stepped out into the cool, pleasant night, a little bell above the door jingled, blending neatly in time with the music from the jukebox.

JULIE LEFT THE DREAMKEEPER'S Emporium with the only plan she felt she could reasonably enact, given the circumstances: *do something different.*

She decided that, no matter what she *felt* like doing, she would simply *do something different*, and see where *that* led. Since none of this really made any sense anyway, it seemed the last thing she could dependably rely on would be *consistency.*

"Okay," she said aloud. "So, I want to find Charley. Which means: I've got to try to avoid finding Charley *at all costs.*"

Step one had been to *leave the Emporium entirely.* The most "reasonable" thing to do would have been to try and find Charley by "guessing" which way he went, weaving her way through the maze of halls and rooms.

"The only place you can get *back* to is the front room of the Emporium?" she surmised, speaking aloud. "Because that's where the checkout counter is?" She frowned, noting the little asphalt parking lot she stood in. The storybook moon seemed almost to grin at her bewilderment, having started its downward turn to one horizon. To her left was a larger, two-way street; past that, a vast parking lot with what looked like a strip mall at the farthest end of it.

"To *not* find someone, I'd need to *avoid* where they would be," she said aloud. "So where the hell would Charley go?"

Julie suddenly realized the extent of her *real* relationship with Charley. Besides his insipid adoration of Molly Furnival, the constant stream of second-rate fiction he was reading, and his association with the Bhairavi Society, she had *no idea* what he was *really* like.

They hadn't been friends before Mike's death and resurrection. Hell, she wasn't even sure if they were *really* friends *now*—they chatted like acquaintances, but never really *about* anything except Fear Club stuff. Not like with Steve—who was a bastard, but still managed to get her birthday presents every year without fail, and Christmas gifts, and was somehow able to cheer her up whenever she failed a test or fell into one of those black moods...

So was *that* why she had confided in Charley about Foxend? Because, basically, he was just a stranger? A fucking *therapist*, even?

She turned around. The giant pyramid that appeared to take up the entire city's center hovered against the backdrop of night sky. *Go* that *way?* she thought—and quickly realized that *that* is *exactly* where Charley would head.

She reversed direction again and started walking, exiting the parking lot and heading away from the pyramid along what appeared to be a main street. The city unfolded, miraculously more beautiful and intricate than even she had initially suspected. After a time, the street widened, revealing alleyways leading off to either side in between the various buildings, which had begun to take on a slightly more modern cast in some respects.

Shop windows began to appear, advertising all sorts of items, which in the dim light illuminating a number of them on the inside appeared to be deeper and taller than they could possibly be, given their dimensions taken from outside. The variety seemed endless and nonrepeating: clothing in fabrics that looked like hybrid variants of silks and cottons and woven threads with jewelry composed of unimaginable varieties of stone, crystal, metal, and even organic materials like feathers, all decked out on finely wrought mannequins; every possible number and type of doll and toy and boardgame and playing-card deck in stacks and on shelves, scat-

tered over tables or arranged in neat rows; a shop
that appeared entirely devoted to different kinds of
flowers in an impossible-to-categorize degree of variety; a tobacconist's paradise (which Julie fought
the urge to investigate further); something that
looked like a little convenience store, with shelf
upon shelf of chocolate bars and candies...

Everything, everywhere, proved utterly and
completely devoid of *people*, just like in the Emporium.

A strange breeze picked up. Julie, shaken from
her reverie, realized she had been walking down
the middle of a thoroughfare with a mall on one
side of it. It appeared as if she was entering a sort
of "downtown" region. A tire place announced its
presence well before she saw it with the pungent
smell of new rubber. A goddamned *used car lot*
sprawled out past the mall. A gas station with
its lights on, up ahead, followed a string of little
hole-in-the-walls with Chinese lettering for signs,
all apparently "closed" at the moment, though the
scent of fried rice and egg drop soup wafted by
briefly.

"I should get a car," she said. "Oh, shit! *Yes.* I
should get a *fucking* car!"

She sprinted over to the car lot.

Where is it...where is it...where is it...

By the glaring light of handfuls of thousand-
watt bulbs overhead, Julie wove her way through
old Toyotas and Volvos, Fords and—*yes*, Hondas,
but not quite—*yes!*

There it sat, keys in the ignition, full tank of gas,
her unpainted 1981 Honda Civic—the "Little Fist,"

Steve sometimes called it, due to Julie's tendency to punch through intersections during the last few seconds of a yellow light. Or the first few seconds of a red one.

She got in and patted the steering wheel. "Okay. We're just going to *drive*," she said. "We're going to head off, and fucking *drive* until we find the *end* of this place. Or until we run out of gas." She started the car. The oddly comforting scent of exhaust smoke arose briefly.

She reached into the glovebox. Her reserve cigarettes. She lit one, put the car in gear, and took off.

ROLAND THE DREAMKEEPER RETURNED to the front of the Emporium a few minutes after Julie left.

"Rolls-Royce!" Steve said, tossing his comic book on the table. "Been a while!"

"Indeed!" Roland replied. "Sorry I missed Julie on her way out. I didn't offend her, somehow, did I?"

Steve waved his hand. "Oh, she's got trust issues. She was afraid to talk to you about Charley."

Roland sat down and began loading a neatly curved black pipe with tobacco from a pouch in his shirt pocket. "That's unfortunate," he said. "What did she want to know?"

"Where the hell he *went*, man!" Steve said. "And I told her I'd ask you when you got back. So I guess here I am, asking you."

Roland smiled and took a few puffs from his pipe. A pleasing aroma of vanilla and honeysuckle emanated from the pipe's mouth. "Charley went back to Golem Creek," he said.

Steve sat up straight. "Are you serious?"

Roland nodded. "Deadly," he said. "And Julie's going to run into him there."

Steve stood from his seat. "How—"

"I am fully aware of *all* of his dreams, Steve," he said. "Laban had to have a failsafe in place before he" —Roland coughed, politely— "*altered.*"

Steve sat back down. "Laban?" he repeated.

Roland nodded. "Laban Black, yes. My maker."

"Huh," Steve said. "Huh."

Roland chuckled. "That pyramid you saw from your room this morning? His tomb. But, gods, what lengths we've all gone to in order to try and keep things sane around here."

"What do you mean?" Steve asked.

"Well, if you haven't noticed," Roland said, switching to an easy chair Steve actually *hadn't* noticed in the room before, "this place is *empty*. I'm not even really a 'person' in the sense you'd normally conceive of it."

"Then what *are* you?" Steve asked.

"I'm this *place*, the *Emporium*," Roland replied, waving his hand in the air. "I am the labyrinth that holds this world in check. Think about it. How do we know an inside from an outside? Can a world exist without an *inside*? What's 'in' your head— does that *oppose* or *somehow support* what appears 'outside' your head?"

Steve ran both hands through his hair and

slumped. "I don't know what the fuck you're talking about," he said.

Roland chuckled again. "Of course you do! Ah, Steve—you sell yourself short."

"All I know is that we got here after kicking that box—"

"Ah, yes, the box," Roland said, raising his eyebrows. "Michael Flowers and his little box. I can tell you this: *I'm glad it was* you three *who ended up here, and not* him."

Steve spoke hesitatingly. "Why?"

"Because if Curwen has somehow succeeded in ensuring Michael's complicity in his plans, then that world of yours 'out there'" —he chuckled again at this— "wouldn't last *two minutes* in the wake of his arrival."

"And why in the hell is that?" Steve tried not to sound overly irritated at Roland's somewhat pedantic manner of speaking. But he was getting *tired* of all this roundabout nonsense.

"He forms the balance," Roland answered simply. "If he were to somehow gain entrance *here*, the gates could be unsealed. Laban's entire plan could be relegated to the dustbin. It is *Michael Flowers himself*, his very *heart*, that can tip the scales. The only thing, in fact. Reasonably enough, Laban never thought it wise to dream such a possibility and actually test it out."

"So..." Steve tried to get a grip on what the Dreamkeeper was suggesting. "This place is—"

"Safe, is what it is," Roland finished for him. "'The Place of Solace.' That's what Laban called it. The untouchable place, in between the worlds.

Laban found the seeds of it when he first investigated the wishing well in Golem Creek—your 'Murk.' But he also found the denizens who dwelt below, and learned of their plans to return to the surface. When the holder of the Silver Key told him, through Curwen, about the *perichoresis of dimensions*, the places where the worlds overlap, he saw immediately the solution—the means of escape!" Roland started laughing again.

"Curwen—Curwen *Flowers*?" Steve rolled his eyes. "Golem Creek town *legends*? I thought Laban Black went back to *England*, or whatever?"

"Not quite," Roland responded. "He went *between*. There *is* a location in your world—several, in fact—from which one can enter the Place of Solace. There are many more ways to get *out* of here. The creatures he had enslaved to build this place for him were banished, true—from *here*. But the gates—the places where the dreams overlap, where what you call 'your' world and the many others that exist or can be dreamed share 'space,' if you will—still allowed for the traversal of some of the denizens of the pit, back and forth. Unless the proper signs and banishings are in place."

Steve paced the room. "What do they want with us, anyway? Those creatures, I mean. It's not *that* great out there!" Steve waved his hands up and around, unsure where to indicate the location of the "usual" world.

"Food sources can dry up," Roland answered. "And...well...let's just say that they are not averse to *human* as a meal replacement."

Steve stopped pacing. "Right," he said, and

shoved his hands in his pockets. "Right. I get it. So is that what happened to Mike? He got 'et,' as they say?"

Roland's pleasant demeanor suddenly diminished. "That I don't know," he said. "Which means he is beyond Laban's dreamings. He tried to take his life once. It is very possible that he has done so again—this time successfully."

Steve was taken aback. "'Tried to take his life once'?" he repeated. "When the hell did he do *that*?"

"The very night you first encountered him, at the hospital," Roland answered. "You and Charles and Julie. After enough of Curwen's instruction, Michael wanted no more of it—the bloody sacrifices, the all-night vigils. When Curwen had first taken him under his wing, Michael thought it the greatest joy. After years of it, though—well, it's quite possible that anyone with some sense, and certainly anyone with a *conscience*, would want out."

"And the only way out was—"

"The end complete. Indeed." Roland puffed on his pipe again. "I don't do fancy things like smoke rings," he apologized. "Forgive me."

Steve began to pace the room.

"I should be *doing* something, then," he said. "Julie—she left! She's back in Golem Creek—with Charley?"

Roland nodded.

"And I'm just *sitting around* here, wasting time—"

Roland shook his head. "I'd hardly call my

DMing 'wasting time'!" he said.

Steve looked slightly apologetic. "You know what I mean!" he said.

"I do, and I'll have you know that there's *no way* you could have wasted any of your time here!" Roland said.

"And how is that?" Steve asked.

"Time doesn't pass, here," Roland answered. "Not in the sense that you normally think of it. Obviously, things are *changing* in here, but *out there* the 'time' button is basically *paused*. I mean, it *can* move 'the usual way' in here, if you *want* it to. But I don't ever really bother with it. I haven't wound a clock in—well, I couldn't technically tell you how long!" He laughed.

"Okay!" Steve brightened. "Then I still have all the time I need!"

"For what?" Roland asked.

"Well, I don't *know*," Steve said. "What do you suggest?"

"Let things take their course," Roland answered. "Another game, perhaps?"

Steve slumped back into his seat.

FIVE MILES IN, PASSING neighborhoods sprawling off in either direction, two parks, and what appeared to be the ruins of a manor house—but still not a single human or animal—Julie tried turning on the radio.

A few twists of the dial, fuzz, static, and then, a voice.

"...all dreaming the same dream." It was a male voice, a little nasal, a little affected. "Whereas we are merely inlets of the One Consciousness—oases, if you will—a temporary respite from Nothingness. When hungry, we eat—the hunger itself is a void, the void triggers the hunger. *Emptiness* is the case— always. And matter is *an escape* from *nothingness*, from emptiness."

The voice paused for a moment. There was a sound like an old TV set tuning in.

"If I may suggest something," the voice went on, "I think you might find it *most enlightening.* Because there *is* a place where time stops, where dreams overlap. And I think, if you can see where I'm going with this, you might want to take the next left at the light."

Julie started. *Did he just—*

"Yes," the voice said. "Next left coming up here... See that side road? Perfect! Take that one down past the stone pillars."

Julie did as the voice suggested.

"What if a god was a key?" it said.

"What?" Julie said out loud. Suddenly, the road up ahead begin to quiver and tremble. No, it wasn't just the road—*it was the air, the sky, the trees—*

Once past it, Julie blinked and shook her head. She was back on the main road. Led Zeppelin's "Black Dog" sounded faintly from the speakers.

She began to slow as she noticed a car stopped on the shoulder of the road up ahead. Charles Leland stood behind it, slamming shut its trunk.

interlude

᠆

THAT
WHICH
REMAINS

Two Years Ago

T HE THINGS OF CHILDHOOD are not *childish*, necessarily," the figure said, its voice a mass of whispers and shadows. "Things become child*ish* when they start getting *sold*. You can always see through the lies of adults. They don't know anything, because they think they know everything."

The figure shifted, intermixing with the darkness.

"And you start to become one of them," it continued. "Why? You start to *believe* their *lies*. There are no explanations for anything. Just more convincing fictions."

Something like mathematical equations began to appear shimmering in the air around it.

"You believe *that*?" it laughed. "So if I change my name to something 'more consistent,' I am somehow more *me*? If I decide this moment to play a different role, but I do it with perfect believability, perfect consistency, that *new* role is somehow...*truer*?"

The silvery numbers and other figures became blurry, misty, and faded back into the darkness.

"Ah, they simply make things up, just like we do," it said. "But their lies only serve to make things *less* wonderful. They make up money...then they make up burdens to make the money seem more believable. They make up jobs...then they make up school and degrees to make the jobs seem more believable. They make up knowledge, they make up 'facts,' they make up *truths*...then they make up argumentation and debate, they make up conflict, to make all of their facts seem less like fiction." It seemed to sigh momentarily. "But the world you live in depends entirely upon *you*, on what fictions you choose to believe in. That is the secret. That is the *key*."

I projected an image of myself into the darkness. The shape within it laughed again.

"The most basic lie of all," it said. "What is a *person*, anyway? What is a *place*? What are *things*? Except appearances, never seen from all possible angles at once, and therefore always mostly mysterious, whether we recognize that Mystery within them or not."

I could sense the capital "M" on the word. Given that most of this conversation was obviously occurring in my head, that wasn't too odd.

I opened my eyes.

The hospital. Day. Morning.

I took a breath.

By the gods, I could breathe.

My fever had apparently broken. I gazed about the hospital room and pulled myself to a sitting position. Was that *energy* I felt? It seemed like an old friend, long unseen, suddenly returning from some strange vacation in the wilderness...

"I see you're feeling better?" the nurse walked in. Lissa, that was her name. "You want to try eating something?"

Yes, I would like to, I thought I said. "Yes, I would like to," I repeated in the real world.

"Good for you!" she smiled. Nurse Lissa—ah, what a glorious lady to meet the day with! Those lovely blonde curls snaking all round and about her smile!

"I'd like to—" I said. This was unpracticed. My throat was clear, my lungs functional. I started again. "May I take a walk?" I asked. Did I have to ask permission?

Lissa laughed. Lovely! "Let's take it one step at a time, Charley, okay?" She was fluffing up the pillows behind me. She smiled, bubbling like orange soda. "First I'll get you some breakfast. Then I'll call your mother, and we can all talk to Dr. Berenger."

I smiled back at her. Yes, nice, thank you. "Yes, nice, thank you," I said.

Lissa bounced out of the room.

I leaned over to my side and gazed out the window. The sun shone, but the wind was clearly blowing. Tree branches and leaves fluttered. I could sense that it was cold. After Christmas? Yes.

Something was sticking into my side. I reached under myself and brought forth a plain Bic pen, ballpoint. Cheap. I gazed at it for a moment.

Someone in the next room was arguing.

"...so fucking broken then how do you explain *this*?"

I heard a thump, and a few gasps.

"Because *I* don't feel a *goddamned* thing. So get this fucker off of me—"

"Steve, please!" A girl's voice. "Your dad's on his way."

Steve snorted. "Like that's going to help."

"Steve, listen," another voice, slightly older, very irritated. "We're going to do another X-ray, okay? If it's fixed, then it's fixed, right? So please just sit down until your dad gets here—"

"Snickers," Steve said.

"What?" the other voice responded.

"Get me a Snickers bar and I'll sit the fuck down," he said.

There was some scuffling, apparently in acquiescence to his request, then the voices died down to mumbling, of which I could make out only every few words.

I held up the pen against a backdrop of trees blowing in the wind outside.

I'm going to use this to write Molly a letter.

"I'm going to use this to write Molly a letter," I said aloud, and closed my eyes, feeling marvelous.

"AMAZING, CHARLEY," MY MOTHER said as she drove me home later that day. "That immune system of yours! Just like your dad's. You know he had meningitis really bad when he was a kid?"

I nodded. I knew the story. Truly, it must be my incredible genetic lineage that resulted in such a miraculous healing.

And I really couldn't explain *why* I felt so phenomenally good—well enough, even, to begin to dread having to return to school after winter break.

"Too bad about that Flowers kid," she continued. "We'll have to go to his funeral, you know. Dad's got connections to that family at work."

I nodded. Poor kid. I guess. Didn't really know him all that well, since he didn't go to public school with the rest of us. Home-schooled, private tutors—it was a big house, I was sure his family could afford it.

I felt as if I should say something, especially since my mother seemed so chatty. "Yeah," I finally said. "Uh—did you hear what happened to him?"

My mother winced. "Nasty stuff," she said. "Some crazy person *stabbed* him! Can you believe it?"

"Why?" I asked.

"Who knows?" she answered. "Crazy people do crazy things."

I gazed out the window at the minimal afternoon traffic. We were passing Maple Ridge Elementary. "Did they catch the guy?" I asked.

"I don't know," she said. "No, I guess. Probably would have heard about it. Which means: you're not going *anywhere* after dark!"

"Did he get stabbed at night?" I asked.

My mother thought for a moment. "Fine," she said. "I don't know. So just don't go anywhere. At least not without somebody else with you. Please?"

I nodded. My thoughts had already returned to the letter I intended to write for Molly.

LATER THAT NIGHT, HAVING assured my mother that I still felt perfectly fine (although I could most certainly do with another few days off of school), I started to do just that, but nothing came out right. I mean literally.

As I attempted to formulate the words "My dearest Molly," this is what took shape:

Jy pbtobqs Jliiy.

"What in the world?" I said aloud. I tried it again—with the same result. I shook the pen a few times, and tried a third time—yet again, the insufferable jumble of nonsense. I tried something different, and very carefully wrote "What the fuck?"

Wets seb cuah?

Indeed, that was the question. As I constructed each of the letters that I intended to write, the pen seemed to somehow metamorphose them into alternate versions. I tried a few more statements:

Qetii F aljmtob sebb sl t qujjbo'q pty?
(Shall I compare thee to a summer's day?)

F'ii sthb t aebbqbruodbo tkp cofbq.
(I'll take a cheeseburger and fries.)

Dobbsfkdq, Aetoibq!
(Greetings, Charles!)

The last one stopped me cold. I had seen it before. I glared at it in the dim yellow light from my nightstand.

Dobbsfkdq, Aetoibq!

"Greetings, Charles," I said aloud. I shifted my gaze to the window near the bed. A horned moon rose over Chicken Hill, outlining the scraggly black branches of trees shorn of their leaves. Greetings, Charles...

Suddenly, it hit me. I knew what to do.

"I know what to do!" I exclaimed aloud, and wrote out the entire alphabet in a neat grid on the sheet of paper.

There, before me, lay the answer, the key—or, rather, the key word. It was so simple, I laughed aloud. "Trap!" I read in place of the letters A, B, C, D. A substitution code—I remembered it from algebra class, when Mr. Gurdjian tried and failed repeatedly to impress us with the great value of modular arithmetic and some of the other basics of number theory.

"You just choose a word—any word—and write it down under the first set of letters in the alphabet," he told us in that nuanced monotone of his. He had been teaching high school for long enough that the robot had taken over a good part of his human essence. "Ideally, choose a word with no repeating letters, to make it easier. Then just fill in the remaining letters of the alphabet underneath the usual alphabet, in their usual order, without repeating any of the letters from your key word."

A substitution code! Wonderful!

The only thing I couldn't explain was how—and perhaps more importantly *why*—this goddamned pen was doing it all by itself. Where had the damned thing come from?

THE STRANGE, DARK FIGURE from my eerie dream of the night before returned as I slept.

"You'll need more than wit to resolve this," it said in fluttering moonlight and silvery shadow. "There are more stakes than you realize."

My frustration and anxiety revealed themselves in a burst of pale, thirsty light.

"I'm doing my best to help you," it responded. "But your story keeps splitting."

A question mark, like a smoke ring, rose into the sky and dissipated.

"Never mind," the figure seemed to expand and contract, as if taking a deep breath or sighing. "At any rate, when you go to the funeral, pay attention to the girl with the purple flower on her dress."

An image of a purple rose bloomed in the darkness, radiating with dark light, then faded again.

THE FUNERAL WAS PECULIAR, to say the least.

Apparently, owing to differences of opinion on the part of his parents (who sat on opposite sides of the room during the service—a tale in itself, I felt sure), Michael Flowers was to be buried with little ceremony. Instead, an extremely weird and (as far as I could tell) utterly unsuitable eulogy was recited in the viewing room at the funeral home by a wild-eyed old man with a tendency to mumble. I had never seen him before.

"We *are* gathered here today" —his choice of which words to emphasize were odd and somewhat off-putting— "to remind *you* that the world, as we know it, often fails us, often rewards those who deserve no reward. Can you imagine *listening* to the radio and assuming that what it told you held true, always? I, myself, considered Michael Flowers an exceptional, a truly *good* person."

I couldn't be the only person having the realization that this man was insane. I glanced about the room. The breath caught in my throat as my dream of a few days ago suddenly came fully into memory once again. A dark-haired girl stood nearly in shadow at the back of the room by a young man who appeared to be roughly my own age. That was...Steve, wasn't it? Right. Steve Chernowski. He was famous for having served nearly two full years' worth of detentions, and even more famous for rarely committing the same infraction twice in order to land himself there.

But what blew my mind was the flower she wore on the lapel of her jacket. A purple rose, identical to the one from my dream...

"Now," the old man continued his convoluted drivel. "It is those whom we *speak* about in memory that live on in our memories. *To* those ones, I say, we must attend, always. It is to *them* that we must sacrifice some of the present for the sake of our own little futures."

He stepped down from the podium and headed directly for the hall leading to the reception room. In the silence following his self-dismissal, I thought I could even hear him pouring himself a drink. No one clapped, of course. No one even moved for several minutes, until the funeral director himself seemed obliged to step up and direct the action elsewhere.

I felt a compulsion, an urge, unstoppable, to get up and run to those two at the back of the room. I was barely able to resist sprinting over to them, and instead stood up rapidly as everyone else began making their way—with painful slowness—to the reception area.

"I'll be right—uh, I'll be right back," I said to my mother, seated beside me, nearly tripping over myself to get away. What had possessed me? I heard my father make some comment—"Where's he running off to?"—before almost knocking over an elderly woman wearing an incredibly elaborate wig of bright red hair.

"Pardon!" I said loudly. She frowned. "Sorry, really—"

As the small crowd of people filtered toward the reception area, I headed the opposite direction. When I looked up from my brief entanglement, I noticed that Steve Chernowski and the purple-rose girl were already heading out.

"Wait!" I yelled. Several people glared at me. I finally made my way to the doors at the front of the building and burst through them, terrified that my quarry had evaporated, that my chance at understanding what in the world was going on would evaporate like so much smoke, like an illusionist's rabbit in a hat, like—

"Dude!" It was Steve Chernowski. "Chill!"

He stepped out of a cloud of smoke in a little alcove outside the building, to the left of the entranceway. The girl was behind him. The smoke was from two cigarettes she held in one black-gloved hand.

She offered one of them to Steve. "Thanks, Jules," he said. "You think this is the guy?"

I stood there, more than perplexed.

"Yep," she said, taking a deep drag on her cigarette and exhaling. "That's him."

"WE HAVE TO DO *what*?"

I felt like a rat between two house cats; they didn't need me for food, but goddamn was I fun.

"Grave. Three nights from now. Meet." It was Steve saying this, sitting in the front seat of Julie's Honda. "Capiche?"

I nodded. "Okay, good," I said. "Because I thought for a moment there you were telling me that I had to sneak into Golem Creek Cemetery in the middle of the night to watch someone rise from the dead."

Steve laughed. "I like him!" he said to Julie, who was intent on the road. "Clever, smart. Let's keep him."

"Look, Charley, I'm sorry if this seems *inconvenient* for you," Julie said, turning into the parking lot of a FazMart. "But do you *realize* the inconceivability of the dreams we both had being *random events*?"

She parked and nodded at Steve, who hopped out of the car as if he knew what to do. Then she turned to look at me.

"What happened at the hospital was effectively a *miracle*," she continued. "And me, you, and—for the love of God—Steve Chernowski are somehow a key part of it. We need to go to the graveyard and we *have to* make sure that Mike Flowers gets out of that coffin, alive and well." She paused for a moment. "At least alive, if not exactly *well*," she said.

"Forgive me if I seem to have reacted incongruously," I said. "I'm new to necromancy."

Julie turned to watch Steve heading back to the car. "Fancy words, kid," she said. "Just fucking be there."

"Fine," I responded. "Fine! Okay?"

Steve got back in the car.

"What'd I miss?" he asked, tossing Julie a pack of Marlboros.

"Charley's in," she said.

"Aw, Julie!" Steve said. "Did you promise to make out with him afterward? She's a fucking liar, Charley. She's been promising me that for *years*."

Julie was shaking her head as she unwrapped the cigarette package.

"I'll be there," I said. "Can you drop me off at Maple Ridge?" I realized how stupid it sounded the minute I said it, and Steve didn't fail to laugh.

"Whatever you want," Julie said, depressing the car lighter and turning on the car.

I JUST NEEDED A place to think, and Maple Ridge was the most peaceful I knew of.

They dropped me off without another word. Here I was, sixteen years old, and the most extraordinary thing I had done so far was win second place in the state science fair. Second place! (That bastard with the four-year study had bested me.)

The offer to do something that basically made me quake in fear to think about was somehow... *comforting.* Years and years of reading nothing but science fiction and fantasy novels made it easier for me to cope with at least the *possibility* of the idea that someone could return from the dead.

Some little kids played soccer a distance away, at the far edge of the big lawn behind Maple Ridge. I eyed the area briefly to ensure that nobody was watching me, and slipped behind the dumpsters to check my old hiding spot behind the false brick.

Neatly folded, just behind the brick and in front of a little baggie of Micro Machines, was a sheet of typing paper, apparently with writing on it.

I withdrew the sheet in terror—*who else knew about the false brick?*

Charley, man, hey, I know this is weird, it read in an unknown, but somewhat artistic, hand. *Didn't mean to compromise your stash, dude, but apparently this is the "only way" to get this to you...*

What in the *world*?

Anyway: check it out. The weird letters on the back of this page? Yeah, you need those. I try to get it to you after English, but you get real caught up in this mess right at that point.

I noticed the unusual tense change of the message.

(That's a shit-ton of time from now!) I guess it's in code so that only you can read it, just in case, so, like in Mission: Impossible, *burn it once you've figured it out. Wish I could be more help! Peace.*

The note was signed "Pete" with a flourish that

included the anarchist "A" symbol and a stylized "t" that looked like a joint on a roach clip.

I took one look at the encoded message on the back of the page, replaced the false brick, and sprinted home.

"GREETINGS, CHARLES!" I READ aloud in the confines of my room. "When you can read this, be sure to get the key on the other side of this message. P.S.: Sorry for the black eye!"

I slumped down in my desk chair. All of the excitement I had been feeling while decoding the message vanished.

I turned the page over and re-read the weird scrawl from "Pete." There was supposed to be a "key" in this? And *what* black eye, again? Not to mention: who the hell was "Pete"?

I set the page down on my desk. Then I started pacing the room.

I try to get it to you after English, but...

This was a message from the *future*?

Someone was knocking at my door.

"Charley?" It was my mother. "Hey, Charley, is everything all right?"

My parents had gotten back from the funeral.

I scrambled to get the message shoved into a desk drawer, then went over and opened the door.

"Yeah, fine," I said. My face was obviously flushed. "I just—yeah, I just didn't—"

"Hey, do you think you're getting sick again?" my mother asked. She put the cool palm of her hand on my forehead. "Maybe you should lie down."

"Naw, mom, I'm fine, I think." I was fumbling for words. This wasn't helping my case.

She let her hand drop. "You know, I guess that was a pretty awful thing," she said. "The Flowers kid, you know."

I retreated back into my room and sat down on the edge of my bed. "Yeah," I said, quickly taking advantage of my way out. "Definitely." I hung my head.

"If you want to talk about it—" she started.

"Naw, I'm good, I'm good," I said, looking up again. "Just want to be alone for a while."

My mother smiled. "Your dad wanted me to yell at you for causing a scene at the funeral," she half-whispered. "Let's say I went ahead and did that, okay?"

I smiled back at her. "Okay," I said.

"Anything you need," she said, raising her eyebrows. I nodded. She closed the door behind her.

"Anything I need," I repeated. I went back to the desk and retrieved the sheet of paper. I would drop it in my dad's industrial shredder once I'd memorized the contents.

What I *needed*, apparently, was a stiff drink, which I'd never previously had nor craved.

"Not an issue," Steve said three nights later. "Here, drink this. It'll warm you up." He handed me a little metal flask. "Make that little scratch feel better, too."

I hesitated, pressing down on the bandage I had wrapped about my left hand. As part of the conditions for the ritual, Julie had made rather deep (I thought) cuts in first Steve's palm, then mine. In typical fashion, Steve had insisted that Julie cut herself as well, a request she ignored as if she hadn't even heard it. We had then both held our hands over a cloth sack (roughly the size of a human body, and filled with *what* I didn't want to know) set over Michael's grave and shook some of our blood onto it, per Julie's instruction.

"Go on, drink it!" he repeated. "I ain't got all day."

"Steve," Julie said in what I had identified as her "usual tone" with him. She seemed a lot more like a tolerant mother than a sixteen-year-old girl with a severe nicotine addiction.

I shrugged and took a swig. *Fire.*

Coughing, I handed the foul contents back to him. "Ah, young man!" Steve said, tipping the flask back. "You fail to appreciate the Amontillado! Curses on thee!" He shook his fist at me. "Curses!"

"Steve!" Julie was lighting the wick of an oil lamp she had set beside Mike's headstone. Already, a small stone bowl of some wicked-smelling herbal concoction was burning in front of it, smoke wafting gently over the tightly cinched cloth sack. The latter appeared to be leaking a dark substance now, an amount far in excess of the blood it had already been sprinkled with.

"Wasn't the Amontillado what he promises the guy he's going to—" I started.

"Guys, let's get focused here," Julie said. "I hope I get these fucking words right." She took out a small sheet of paper and reviewed it by the dim light of the oil lamp. The wind was starting to pick up.

I glanced out over the little valley below. In the darkness, you might almost believe that the gravestones peppering the area were tiny dancing shadows, all gathering to witness the strange rite on the hill where we stood.

She produced a dark green wine bottle out of the black bag and pulled out the cork. "Okay," she said.

"Woah," Steve said, suddenly interested in the proceedings. "Pass that on over here—"

"Trust me," Julie said flatly. "You *don't* want what's in here."

Steve frowned dramatically.

"Now. Just *can* it for a few minutes, okay?" She was looking directly at Steve as she said this. He smiled and shrugged with mock innocence.

Julie gazed at the bag set over the grave of Michael Flowers, and began to mumble something under her breath. Within seconds, the temperature dropped substantially. I began to shudder. Even Steve appeared uncomfortable.

I pulled the hood of my black wool jacket over my head.

Julie's eyes closed. The oil lamp began to flicker, and smoke from the burning herbs began spinning tornadically this way and that in the weirdly uncertain breeze. What in the world was she mumbling? It almost began to seem like it was *echoing* throughout the graveyard.

Slowly, she began to pour the contents of the bottle over the cloth sack. I could hear part of what she was saying, now; something like: "*Mortui vivos docent! Mortui resurgent!"*

The bag began to move, as if there was something in it. I stared, terrified, riveted.

Julie continued to chant for a few moments more, and after emptying the contents of the bottle on the sack, a pale, purplish-mauve *radiance* began to emanate from it. She stepped back as the luminosity grew.

My eyes widened in astonishment. This was just like a scene in a *horror movie*—what had I just stumbled upon? Who the fuck *were* these people? Dreams of weird creatures were one thing—but *actual resurrections from the dead?*

The luminescence became stronger, and the contents of the sack began to *writhe* and *moan*. In stark terror, I chanced a look at Steve; he was literally standing there on the other side of the grave, frozen in place, eyes agape, mouth open in astonishment.

Julie was clearly in some sort of trance. She slumped down to her knees on the ground, eyes half-lidded, gazing impassively at the cosmically un-fucking-believable event transpiring before us all.

The bag began to shred. Light escaped from the bag like a luminescent fluid, pouring out onto the earth around it, which appeared to heave slightly in response, as if quenching its thirst after a long drought.

There was a final blaze of light, so bright I had to shield my eyes from it.

When I opened them again, it was to see a lean and muscular figure, naked and soaked in blood, standing in the place where we had all been looking a moment ago. The wind had died down. Silence returned.

Michael Flowers gazed down at his hands, then at the full moon in the sky above. Somehow, I knew that he was utterly aware of our presence—an aura of *total control* radiated from him, dominating the situation in its entirety. Julie rose up, suddenly bearing a large swathe of dark cloth, which she draped over him as he raised his arms. With his face covered in blood, he looked like some mad, cowled monk.

"Well then," he said without taking his eyes off the sky. "Let's begin our lessons, shall we?"

AND THUS BEGAN WHAT Mike called the Bhairavi Society. The monthly lectures...the secrecy...the Ordeals...we basked in it, we absorbed it, and—whether or not we could actually *trust* Mike—we *got stronger.*

All the while, I kept my knowledge of the message from "Pete" utterly to myself. I hid the pen at the back of one of my desk drawers. I tried writing out the *other* side of the sheet as I had memorized it—the side that seemed comprehensible initially—with the "magic pen," but all I got was garbled nonsense.

I was frustrated, yet something intangible kept me from relaying any information about the affair to anyone else in Fear Club—especially Mike Flowers.

But everything changed on the night of Amanda Whitfield's party.

part three

QUICK FIX

WHEN I SAW THE grid of letters reproduced in the little journal, embers of memory suddenly erupted like an inferno.

...Steve snorted. "So obvious," he said.

"*Wait* a second here." I said. I stood up slowly from my seat at the patio table in the backyard of Amanda Whitfield's house. "I *know* this."

The party rang out in full force just around the corner. Something battered at my conscious awareness as I read the uncanny journal I had removed from the box in the Murk. Like the sensation you get *just before* something truly terrible happens.

"What are you talking about?" Julie said.

"You mean that you—" Steve said.

"Yes," I said, pointing at the grid of letters in the little book. "*Yes*. I can *read* this!"

"So what the fuck does it say?" Steve said.

I hesitated for a moment. "It says—" I stopped. "Oh, my God." As I rehearsed the words in my mind, the floodgates opened. I saw what was about to happen—or, at least, I *began* to see it with increasing clarity, as each moment passed.

I grabbed Steve by the shoulder. "*We've got
to get the fuck out of here!*" I whispered harshly.
"*Right now!*"

Julie was up already. I grabbed the key and
shoved both it and the book into my jacket. We
started back toward the party. And that's when
I saw the "wolfman" again, in the John Travolta
getup, dancing in the midst of the crowd.

"Shit!" I backed against a wall. Julie and Steve
seemed to sense the seriousness of the situation
and followed suit.

"Dude!" Julie said. "What the *fuck*—"

"That guy's about to kill someone!" I tried to
keep my voice down and my wits about me.

Steve glanced around the corner. "*Which* guy?"
he said.

"The wolfman!" I said.

Steve turned to Julie. "I think our boy's finally
lost his shit—"

"Steve! I'm fucking *serious*!" I said. "Can we
save her?" I was frantic now. "Oh, *shit*. Molly.
Molly's about to come around the corner."

Julie peeked around the corner. "Holy *shit*,
Charley!" she said. "She's right over there. She
just headed out the back door—"

My mind was racing. Save Molly? Save the wolfman's dance partner. Diversion? *The bat-winged
creature on the roof of the house...the four monster
hunters...*

I knew what to do. At least, it seemed like our
only chance.

I grabbed Steve by both shoulders. "*Don't follow me,*" I said. "You and Julie *go grab Molly.*

Fucking *kidnap* her if you have to. Then go *that way*" —I pointed to the side of the house— "to get to the car. And *don't go back to the fucking party.*"

I shook him once to show him I was serious. He nodded. I sprinted for all I was worth to the back fence and over it without a second glance.

ABOUT TWENTY YARDS OF lawn lay beyond the fence from the street, where the monster hunters' Pontiac 6000 was already rumbling toward me. I ran directly for it. They screeched to a halt.

"Werewolf!" I yelled as I ran up to the window. I bent over double for a second and retched.

"Woah, dude," the long-haired guy who was driving said. "What's up? Are you all—"

"Werewolf! Killing girl! Please!" I pointed, then retched again.

THE AMAZING THING ABOUT monster hunters is, I guess, the speed with which they can mobilize when their life's work is at stake.

I collapsed to the ground briefly, and one of them—the guy who had been working the camera—came over to check on me. The driver had taken one more quick look at me, then extracted a handgun from within his army-issue jacket, cocked it, and leapt out of the car. He and two of the others were practically at the fence before I could even rasp out my name. The guy who had been working the video camera knelt down by me.

"My name's Fitz," he said. "How many fingers am I holding up?"

I gazed at a black-gloved hand holding up three fingers against the glow of an orange street-lamp. "Um—" I said.

"Good. Can you get up?" He offered me a hand. I grabbed it and unsteadily began to pull myself up. Gunshots rang out from the direction of the party.

I collapsed again.

"Hey, it's all right," Fitz said. "No one's gonna get hurt. We're on it." He lifted me up and leaned me against the car. "We *are*, however, going to need to get the fuck out of here in about sixty seconds. I figure, nice ritzy neighborhood like this, cops'll probably take no less than a minute to get out here." He laughed. "Rich bitches in trouble? Oh, you bet your fucking *ass* they don't want to be handing out any goddamned suspensions!"

I heard car engines revving and tires screeching from the direction of the house. Some general commotion. No further gunshots, though.

He pulled out a handgun. "This will get you in trouble with the law," he said, cocking it. "It will also get you *out* of trouble when the law ain't around." He laughed again. "Can you breathe?"

I could breathe. "Yeah," I said. "I can breathe."

"After you," he said, opening the car door.

As soon as I got in, Fitz's cool demeanor became focused intensity. We were swerving around the corner toward the front of Amanda's house about thirty seconds later.

One of the other hunters was already waiting in the circular driveway out front.

"What took you so long?" he said.

"Dead weight," Fitz said, jerking his thumb back at me. He laughed. I cringed. Fitz had popped the trunk and the other hunter rummaged through it briefly.

I noticed with relief that Julie's Honda was gone. A number of doors and windows on the house were flung open, but not a soul was in sight. Lights burned everywhere. I noticed with chagrin that I could still hear music from within the house, dimly. I noticed with even *more* chagrin that it was still the fucking Bee-Gees.

Seconds later, the other three hunters emerged from the party. Two of them ran fore and aft of *a body bag*—

"Um, did you guys—" I said.

Fitz looked at me in the rear-view mirror. "Yup," he said. He put the car in gear.

"Let's go, let's go, let's *go*!" shouted the long-haired guy, leaping into the front seat. The other two crowded in beside me after dumping their corpse into the trunk and slamming it shut.

We peeled out just as sirens became painfully noticeable. Everyone in the car was silent, breathing heavily. The guy next to me smelled like fresh dirt and cap-gun smoke.

Fitz seemed to drive brilliantly, on instinct, and even cut directly across a small playground at one point, emerging onto a larger street that fed out the other end of the neighborhood. In a few moments, we were clear of the neighborhood itself. Fitz pulled up to a red light on one of the Forty Winks main streets and stopped.

"Back to Pete's for a midnight snack?" he asked.

"Can't," said the long-hair. "Pete's dead. We just killed him."

"PETE'S *DEAD*?" I REPEATED. It had to be—it certainly was—the "Pete" who had written me the note. Who else? Before *this* had happened, the connection would have been maybe arbitrary—but *now*?

The long-haired guy turned to look at me and nodded. "Took me by surprise, too. Pete Jarry! A fucking *werewolf*. Can you believe it?"

"I—" I didn't quite know what to say. Pete— the stoner kid from English class—*Stek's brother, of* course... "Are you *sure*?"

"Well, that's what he said," the long-hair insisted. "I pulled the gun on him. He drops that body he was munching on and starts waving his hands. 'It's Pete!' he yells at me. 'Pete Jarry! Don't shoot! I can control it!'"

The other two hunters were nodding their heads in agreement.

"That's what they all say," he continued. How many times had they done this?

He finally introduced himself. "Booker Reuchlin," he said. "Who are you again?"

"I'm Charles—"

"Head back to rendezvous," he interrupted, speaking to Fitz. "And try to avoid the main streets?"

Fitz nodded.

"Charles?" Booker turned back to me. "That's Barton next to you," he said, pointing. "That's Staley." They both waved. "Now tell me," he continued, "just how the fuck you knew we were going to be there?"

"It's kind of a long story," I said. The sensations of foreknowledge I had experienced at the party had begun to fade. It felt like something substantial had changed—like whatever timeline I had experienced before had now been irrevocably altered, and the usual future randomness or fate or whatever had kicked back in. "What do you want to know?"

"Well, we've got about eight minutes," Booker said. "So give me the eight minute version."

"Okay," I said. "Um—"

"Let's make this easier," he said. "Do you know Michael Flowers?"

My eyes widened. I nodded.

"Do you know where he is *right now*?" he asked.

I shook my head. "No—I mean, I don't think so—"

"You don't *think* so?" he said.

"I mean," I said, "he could be back at the Brake Street house?"

Booker looked over at Fitz, who nodded without skipping a beat.

"Good news, then," Booker said. "We've got to dump this body. May he rest in peace. And we've got to stab Mike Flowers to death—"

"*Wait* a second," I said. "Why do you have to—"

"You want out of this dream? Back to your real life?" Booker said.

I breathed anxiously for a moment. "What do you mean?" I asked.

"This is very simple," Booker said. "Golem Creek isn't real. It's just a made-up place. Which means *you* may very probably be just made up, too. Do you want to find out?"

I didn't quite know what to say. I glanced at Barton, then Staley. They both sat silently staring ahead, as if this was routine conversation.

"I—" I started.

"When we get to Brake Street—" Booker began.

"*No!*" I yelled. "Shut *up*, goddamnit, for one *goddamned fucking second!*"

Silence.

"All right," I said. "So, you're telling me I may not *exist*—"

"Right, that's—" Booker interrupted.

"Shut *up*!" I said again. "Please."

He fell silent again.

"Maybe I don't *want* to find out if I'm not *real*, you know?" I said. "I mean, you're not offering me much of an option."

"It's like the fucking *Matrix*, man!" Booker said. "We're from Tulsa—and that's physical *reality*. This 'Golem Creek' place is just some weird blip in the cosmos."

"How do you *know* that?" I asked. "What if fucking 'Tulsa'—wherever the fuck that is—turns out to be the 'fake' place? Huh? What happens then?"

"Then we *party*!" Booker said. He laughed.

"Do the rest of you agree with him?" I asked, looking at the two beside me.

"Well," Staley said. "Mostly. But one thing's for sure: we've got to find this Mike Flowers guy.

He's the key."

I began to realize that I sat in a carload of crazy people—maybe even just plain, old murderers. These guys weren't "monster hunters"—they were just *hunters*. They even expected me not to care whether their actions destroyed Golem Creek, destroyed *me*.

"Look," I said. "Can we just—"

Thumping, from the trunk.

The hunters immediately tensed and reached for their weapons. Fitz sped up briefly, turned into the next side road, and parked the car under the shade of a willow tree. It looked like we were on a private lane that probably led to someone's property some distance away.

Everyone fell silent.

Thumping, again.

Everyone but Fitz filtered out of the car. I hung my head briefly before stepping out as well, standing off a ways to the side, my heart hammering in my chest. I *really* didn't want to see them shoot anything, even if it was a werewolf.

The three of them were pointing handguns at the trunk.

"Now?" Fitz said out the window, his hand on the driver's side trunk latch.

"Do it," Booker said.

Then a voice, muffled, from within.

"Dudes! Dudes? Hey! Oh, man, this sucks."

They lowered their weapons, all sighing with relief.

"Trunk of a car? I guess. Dark in here," the voice continued strangely.

"Hang on there, Fitz," Booker said. "Don't open it yet."

"Yo! Out there! Hey, it's Pete. Is anybody out there?"

"It's Booker," he said. "Pete? We're going to open the trunk now. Okay?"

"Go for it, man," Pete said. Booker made a motion to Fitz, who reached for the trunk latch.

I heard Pete speak as the trunk unlatched. "Wait—what was that?"

The trunk popped open.

A split second later, Barton lay on the ground with his throat ripped out. The snarling beast had launched out of the trunk, claws and fangs at the ready, growling and biting and tearing at anything in its path. Fitz leapt out of the car and fired at the beast just as Staley did. Both of them appeared to miss—but Staley's miss was fatal. The beast's claws were in his chest moments later, tearing him apart.

Fitz aimed again. "C'mon, you fucker!" He fired once, twice, three times. The creature was obviously hit, its body responding to each bullet. It turned to face Fitz. I noticed that Booker had fallen by the beast, half of his face torn off.

As the creature howled with glee, leaping toward Fitz, I unfroze and dove into the driver's seat of the car.

A second or two later, I was on the main road again, pedal to the floor, the haunting howl of Pete the "Werewolf" fading off in the distance.

I FINALLY HAD TO pull over to close the goddamned

trunk.

As terrifying as the situation was, I felt I had gained sufficient distance from the corpses of my "saviors" to merit the action—not to mention the fact that I had no desire to attract the equivalently unwelcome attention of the Golem Creek police force.

After slowing to a stop on the shoulder of the road, I waited for a few moments, straining my ears listening for any trace of demonic growling or howling or whatever over the low rumble of the Pontiac 6000's engine. At last, I risked turning off the car and stepping out.

I felt lucky, at least, that most of the blood and gore from the monster hunters seemed to have missed the car. What little there was had been obscured by dust and dirt from the road during my frantic escape.

Reluctantly, I removed my jacket, shoved the book and the key into my pants pocket, and buffed all the areas of the car that I was certain I had touched. Once again, there were motivations *other* than the supernatural that I had to address; I would need to ditch the car before getting back to the city proper, but I could at least try to avoid the brunt of any murder charges that went along with grand theft auto, should it come to that.

I could hear some cars up ahead at the highway turnoff. Thankfully, this direction remained obscured in darkness, at least for the moment, but my luck couldn't possibly hold out for long—against civilians, cops, *or* creatures of the night.

I made my way back to the trunk and was

about to slam it shut when I heard, very distinctly, something unexpected.

"Led Zeppelin?" I said aloud.

Car headlights suddenly illuminated the road from behind me. I slammed shut the trunk.

Julie Evergreen pulled up.

"Julie!" I shouted the instant I saw her.

She reached across to roll down the passenger-side window.

"You should probably wipe your prints off that car," she yelled. "I mean, if you stole it. Like you obviously did."

I nodded excitedly. "Holy *shit*, Julie!" I exclaimed. "My *God* you're not going to believe a *single* fucking thing I tell you in the next five minutes!" I took one more quick glance into the Pontiac and noted two backpacks in the backseat, which I extracted.

"*The bags*!" Julie shouted. "Give 'em here!" I obliged her. She handed me a stack of Taco Bell napkins in exchange.

"For old times' sake," she said. I looked at her questioningly. "Never mind," she said. "Hurry up."

"Oh!" I said. "Prints. No—I already did it. See?" I held up my filthy jacket and tossed it into the Honda.

"Wonderful." Julie wrinkled her nose. I hopped into the passenger seat of the Honda, unable to hide my joy at seeing her.

"Let's *drive*!" I said. "Wolfman on the *loose*!"

Julie didn't need to be told twice. We were out on the road again in minutes.

"Thank the gods you found me!" I felt a small

victory for the coincidence. "Where the hell is Steve? Where's Molly?"

"What do you *mean*?" Julie said. "Steve's back at the fucking Dreamkeeper's place. And I hate to break it to you *again*, but Molly's probably fucking *wolfmeat*, man."

I was stunned. "What—Dreamkeeper? What the hell?"

Julie let out a moan. "Oh, man, please don't tell me this is the scene where you've lost your *fucking memory*."

I opened and shut my mouth. Several times. "It's—not?"

"Argh!" Julie slammed a fist against the steering wheel. "What's the last thing that happened? Or maybe even back up a little bit."

I told her. She groaned at regular intervals.

Then *she* told *me*.

"Oh," I finally said. As she told me things, I somehow eerily "remembered" them, as if I had been *dreaming* them while doing other things *here*, awake. "So—I'm a little out of the loop," I concluded for her. "But not really."

Julie nodded. We ended up in the parking lot of an all-night Lots-a-Burger near Golem Creek's modest downtown.

"Gods be *damned*," she said. "I should have known. Wolfman, check. Demons, check. *Two goddamned Steve Chernowskis*?" She let out a long breath. "Should have just stayed in that little room with the Sherlock Holmes pipe."

"What room?" I asked.

"Never mind," she said.

IN ADDITION TO TELLING Julie about the very few things she did *not* already know, I made sure to tell her what the encrypted message in the book actually said.

"The *book!*" she exclaimed. "You *have* it?"

"Yeah, right here," I said, extracting it from the pocket of my jeans. "And this key."

Julie gasped. "Then we've got *everything!* Or, at least, copies of stuff." She proceeded to inform me of the unlikelihood that *this* book and *this* key had any sort of real powers associated with them. At least according to her appraisal of the situation.

"But we don't know for sure," I said.

Julie shook her head. "I'm willing to bet," she said. "But that message. That's something. That's something we can use."

"How is that?" I asked. "It tells me there's a key—I've already *got* one of those—behind 'this' message. Behind *what* message? There's no university here in Golem Creek! So where do we find the 'trap' door?"

Julie smiled, starting the car. "There's no university *here* in Golem Creek," she said. "But *back there*" —she jerked her thumb behind her, pointing down the road we'd been on— "I bet there is."

Julie pulled out of the Lots-a-Burger parking lot and headed back the direction we came.

"What the hell are you *doing?*" I practically screamed. "You're heading *right back* to where all the problems are!"

"Calm down!" she said. "We drive back through that spot where the 'portal' or whatever it is kicked me out. We can find our way back to the Dreamkeeper's Emporium from there."

I was shaking my head. "I don't think this is going to work," I said.

"And why the hell not?" she asked.

"Because—I don't know," I said. "I mean, *I* drove from that direction. And I wasn't in fucking dreamland."

Julie was silent. I shut up. We passed the Pontiac 6000. We kept driving. I gazed up at the moon starting its descent to the other horizon.

We kept driving. Julie turned onto a side road and drove past a pair of stone posts flanking it. Our driving continued without interruption, although my nervousness increased as we passed the spot where the monster hunters had been massacred. *Something's wrong here...*

I finally spoke up.

"Is something supposed to let us know if we're there?" I asked.

Julie was clearly miffed. "I thought so," she said. "I guess not."

"Okay, that didn't work," I said. "How about going back to the Brake Street house? We try kicking the box again, like you told me. That *definitely* worked, right?"

Julie nodded. "Fine," she said. She slowed and proceeded to turn the car around.

"Wait a second," I said. "Hang on."

"What is it?" she asked.

"The bodies!" I exclaimed, realizing the source of the problem I'd noticed earlier. "I saw those monster hunters get practically *shredded* right in front of me! *Where are the bodies?*"

part four

THE
SILENT
GOBLIN
GANG

JESUS *CHRIST*, DUDE!" I yelled out, clutching my hands to my face. "I think you *broke my nose!*"

We were in the hovel behind the Brake Street house. Steve shook out his fist in front of me.

"Fuck!" he said. "I'm *sorry*, man! How the hell was I supposed to know—"

"Maybe *pay attention*?" Julie said. "You know, if you're going to *attack* someone—"

"Calm *down*, hotpants!" Steve said. "I had to be *sure*."

I leaned up against the wall. There was the box, in the center of the room, open.

"Sure of *what*, exactly?" Julie asked.

"He could have been *Mike*!" Steve said, pointing at me. "I *had* to take him out!"

I tried to take in a breath, and coughed. Blood spewed out of my mouth onto the floor.

"Gross," Julie said. She turned back to Steve. "Sorry to ask such a basic question, but: which Steve are you?"

Steve stepped back a pace. "Excuse me?" he said. "What?"

"I mean," Julie continued, "did 'I' just drop you off here, and take Molly home?"

"Yeah," he said. "That was the plan. Right?"

I tried breathing again. A little less blood this time. That seemed good.

Julie sighed. "Right," she said. "Okay, Steve. Here's what you need to know: there's two of you at this moment. One of you slid into an alternate dimension after kicking that box. I'm pretty sure he's still there, right now, playing D & D with some old guy."

Steve smiled. "All right," he said. "I can't blame you for wanting to get double-teamed by the coolest guy in town, Jules, but—"

Julie made a sound of disgust. "Oh, shut *up*, Steve," she said. Steve was laughing. "Look, we *do* need to find Mike. And I'm guessing the other *me* will be here pretty soon. Since I can't think of anything much better than having at least *two* intelligent, capable people trying to find him, we're going to wait for her. Me. Her."

She pulled out a cigarette. Steve was still laughing. He came over to me and held out a hand to help me up.

"Sorry, dude," he said. "I guess I meant that punch for the ol' ball-and-chain there."

Julie stomped over to the back window of the shed and glared at it.

"*STEVE!*" Two Julies sang out in unison, their combined irritation flowing over him like blood from a wound.

Steve could barely contain himself, a torrent of potentially suicidal commentary bubbling up in his mental cauldron. I gazed at him pleadingly—*not now*, I mouthed.

My sinuses still ached from the unpracticed punch given earlier, and my voice rose hollowly. "Can we *please* get on with this?"

Steve shrugged. It had taken some time to calm down the initial shock of the arrival of Julie Two, at least for me and Steve. I found it eerie—yet somehow fitting—that they seemed to acknowledge one another's presence without feeling the need to even introduce themselves. Julie One had insisted— and her "twin" had agreed—that they ought to spend some little while making sure that *everyone* knew what was going on before taking any specific actions. The opinion of Julie Two, and the wise counsel of Julie One, both accorded that, in *this* timeline, kicking the box ought still to send us back to the Dreamkeeper's Emporium, since it hadn't technically happened yet.

"And since it happened the last time—" Julie One said.

"—we can bet on it happening again," Julie Two finished.

It was remarkable seeing the two of them, both dressed identically in jeans and dark shirts, both in the same black hoodie. I even noted that both Julies' Converse seemed knotted identically, a single bunny ear flopping over to the right.

"But before you kick it—" Julie Two continued.

"—let's make sure we have the *stuff* with us,"

said Julie One. "Since—"

"—we ended up with everything we were *wearing*, at least—"

"—the first time."

"Okay?"

They didn't even seem fazed by each others' presence, nor by their telepathic link. I supposed it would be like having your mirror image suddenly externalize...but did she—

"Hey," Steve said, "if I pinched *one* of you" — both Julies scowled at him simultaneously— "no, *seriously*! If I pinched *one* of you, would the *other* one feel it, too? And I haven't seen you guys shake hands yet!"

Both Julies conveniently ignored him, seeming intent to *avoid* touching each other, perhaps *specifically* because Steve had suggested it.

"Can I have one of your Hondas?" Steve asked smirking.

"*No*," both Julies responded. "But you can" — Julie Two started— "go get the bags out of mine," Julie One said.

He looked to both of them once more. "A gain and a loss," he said as he strode out the door. "It's like having exactly one Julie, just twice as hot!"

"All right," I said. "I guess I'm ready for this."

Both Julies nodded. "By the way," began Julie One as soon as Steve was out the door, "both of us *can* feel what happens to one of us."

They smiled at me. "But don't tell Steve," Julie Two said.

I smiled back. "You're great, Julie," I said. "Honestly, I don't know what I'd do without you."

Their grins widened as Julie Two offered Julie One a smoke.

No one quite understood the mechanism by which we were "teleported" into that Other Place. Steve insisted that it was top-secret ultra-dimensional trip wire attached to the bottom of the box. Whatever it was, it worked just as it had the first time.

When I awoke in the hotel room, I remembered it *instantly*. The sensation was one of having been *asleep* before I arrived; somehow, here, in the "dream" place, I was "awake" again. Access to my memories of when I had last been here seemed complete—along with everything else in the other "time streams" I had experienced.

I instantly felt some anxiety about returning to Golem Creek in this regard, as I assumed I eventually would. Would it all fade away again? Would my waking mind just forget it all *again*? Or was it only traversing that particular EXIT from the Christmas-themed department store which would delete it?

I heard voices in the lobby area. Quickly, I got dressed (*again*, I thought), noting as I did so that my nose no longer seemed "broken" (if, indeed, it ever had been). I gazed out the window of the room, and there it was: the pyramid, standing aloof from the whole scene, secure in its own obscurity.

When I entered the lobby area, it was to *one* Steve, *one* Julie, and Roland the Dreamkeeper, all sitting around a circular table with coffee, gourmet donuts, and a large drawing of a pyramid splayed out on it.

"Hey," I said. "How is it that everyone else wakes up before me?"

"She's ready to head into that pyramid," Steve said, ignoring my question.

"Okay," I said, unsure how to proceed. "Before I ask why we'd do that, what happened to the other Julie? And the other Steve, for that matter?"

Steve grimaced. "I never got to meet *me*, dude," he said fretfully. "Apparently, you've got to be *out there*" —he pointed in a few random directions— "in order to split like that."

"Seems more likely you would be able to split *in* a dream, right?" I said.

I noticed Roland raise his eyebrows and wink at me before Julie turned and spoke.

"Roland's pretty sure that the key you've got ought to get us at least into the grounds of Golem Creek University," she said.

"The university's here?" I said.

"Well, kind of," she said. "We'll be a little bit on our own once we're in there, since that particular dream isn't entirely in Roland's head."

I was a little baffled. "I'm not—um—" I said, looking at Roland. He smiled at me.

"This place *is* Roland," Steve said. "I mean, it's not *his* dream—but he *is* the dream. Get it?"

I didn't, exactly, but I decided not to argue.

"Some places overlap," Julie said. "Dreams with waking; dreams with other dreams."

"Oh," I said. "So, when I went to *that* place, before—the *other* Golem Creek—and woke up *from there*, I—"

"Didn't remember this place," Julie finished. "Right. Like how most people forget their regular dreams."

"All right," I said. "Wonderful. So we get into GCU, we get the *other* key, and then—wait, *how precisely* are we supposed to get to GCU without forgetting who we are?"

Everyone turned to look at Roland, who gazed sheepishly back.

"I can't exactly guarantee that such a thing *won't* happen," he finally said. "However, it's my suspicion that we can *safeguard* the procedure, to some extent."

"How's that?" I asked.

"With an *anchor*," he answered.

"An anchor," Julie repeated. "Okay. You mean like a talisman, of some sort?"

"Indeed!" Roland said excitedly. "For example, the *pen* I gave to Charles initially not *only* provided him with the ability to translate dream-messages. It was also enough of *this* dream—*my* dream—to allow me to communicate with him in the alternate timeline."

The memory of strange communications from a dream figure of years ago came back to me. "That was *you* all that time ago?" I said.

"Doing my best to help!" he said.

"But then Julie—and the resurrection spell—" I said, trying to put it together. "How did you get into *her* dreams? She didn't have an anchor." I turned to Julie. "You didn't have an anchor, did you?"

Julie shook her head. "Nope," she said. "I only

met this guy the other day. Or whatever."

Roland actually frowned at this point. I saw that it was difficult for him; his muscles didn't seem to want to do it.

"I'm not the *only* one who can do what I do," he said. "There are others."

"You're saying that Julie's dreams *weren't* from you?" I said.

Roland nodded. "Unfortunately," he said. "My suspicion is that it was Curwen's doing. When you absorbed Michael's essence at his demise, at the hospital, you all became susceptible to his magic."

"Like Mike's curse got transferred to us," Steve said.

"That's one way of putting it," Roland said. "At any rate, I fear that the instruction Julie received in her dreams was of a sufficiently—well, *darker* variety than anything I would have considered appropriate."

Julie looked to me and Steve, then back to Roland. "So what you're saying is—"

Steve chuckled. "He's *saying* that it's *all your fault*, Julie!" he said.

Julie gave Steve her usual sour look. "Oh, right!" she said sarcastically. "Of course. Because you weren't *anywhere to be found* throughout *all* of this. Asshole."

Steve's smile faded. "Touché, mon frère," he said in bad French. "Or whatever."

"Guys, I think this is an opportune time to fucking *drop* the blame and guilt routines, okay?" I suggested. "Roland, do you have pens for them too?"

He stood up from the table and rubbed his hands together. "Better than pens!" he said. "I'll be right back!" He jogged out of the room.

"That guy's pretty spry for being like a million years old," Steve said.

"I still want to know what we do when we get back from GCU," I said. "*If* we get back."

"Well, other than *not* falling asleep when we're there—" she answered.

"Or blowing up," Steve cut in.

"Right. Or blowing up. Then we get back *here* and unlock that pyramid," Julie said.

"What's in the pyramid?" I asked.

"It's Laban Black's tomb!" Steve said excitedly. "Can you believe that shit?"

"Exactly," Julie said. "But we need that *other* key—the one made entirely of dream-stuff—to get in there. Roland sketched us a map of what he knows." She indicated amidst the items on the table a brilliant pen-and-ink masterpiece on one large sheet of paper, displaying the cross-section of a pyramid with some tunnels and rooms visible in the midst of it. There were also some clearly delineated blank spots.

"What are those?" I asked, pointing to one of them.

"Parts that he can't see," Julie said.

Beneath the sketch I saw the map from the little palm-size journal, unfolded and held down with pewter D & D figurines. I leaned over it and pointed to the triangle shape labeled "L.B."

"Laban Black's tomb," I said. "So he *didn't* go back to Wales?"

"He made it *look* like he did," Julie said.

"But then he had a bunch of hell-creatures build this place for him," Steve continued, "and he set it up as a 'safe place' to retreat to."

"Retreat?" I asked. "From what?"

"Those demons, those monsters," Julie said, "that used to come out of the Murk? That was just like a trickle before a flood. The magic spells and evocations and stuff? Like in medieval grimoires? Those were ways of making *cracks* in the astral fabric of the world, to let certain demons in."

"So when *enough* people make *enough* cracks—" Steve started.

"The dam breaks," I finished. "And we get flooded." I recalled my experience in the wishing well. "I should have known."

"Right," Steve said.

"So Laban made a place, a safe place to go, if the world went all to shit," I said.

"Indeed," Roland chimed in, striding back into the room. He carried a grocery bag in both hands before him. "But he was wise enough to provide a few failsafe mechanisms, hidden deep within his dreaming." He set the bag down on the table.

"His dreaming," I repeated. "But that means..."

"Yes," Julie said. "He's *in* that pyramid. Right now. But he's asleep."

"A magical sleep," Roland said, "which he induced just prior to death, to avoid death."

My mind was reeling. *A magical sleep, to avoid death.* "Okay, great," I said. "Got it. Does someone want to tell me what we're supposed to do when we get in there?"

"Oh, right," Steve said. "Sorry. Roland's pretty sure that we can stop Mike from ever getting through and blowing up the dam if we somehow use that key."

"Where's Mike?" I asked.

Everyone shook their heads.

Roland looked truly apologetic. "Beyond my powers," he said. "Michael appears to be shielded, somehow. Cloaked. After returning from his initial demise, I have been utterly unaware of him."

Steve got up from the table and headed over to a couch in the corner, where he began urgently packing a bag with wrapped sandwiches, Cokes, and multiple packs of cigarettes that lay strewn out around it.

"Who the hell knows how long this is gonna take?" he said. "Gotta prepare!"

"These ought to suffice, as anchors," Roland said, reaching into the bag. "I'm guessing that these items could probably demonstrate additional powers in the other worlds." I noted that he made the word plural. "Just like the pen I gave to Charles. Tangential magical phenomena are actually quite a fascinating study. One fellow from Golders Green has written a treatise dealing in part with this—"

"Graxx!" Steve dashed back to the table as Roland placed an inch-tall pewter figurine of a D & D character on it.

"Especially for you, Steve!" Roland said as Steve gingerly lifted the figure into the air, gazing lovingly at it.

"And for you, m'lady," Roland said, handing a small, yellow rectangle to Julie. "May it be a light to you in darkness!"

Julie smiled and turned the lighter over. A look of delighted surprise came over her features. "This is a fucking *Soloviev* fabergé! Do you *realize* how valuable this is?" She shook a cigarette out of a pack from her pocket, and lit it. The flame gleamed instantly, brightly.

Roland was beaming. "I thought you'd like that," he said. "More importantly, I need you each to have something that you *won't lose.*"

He presented me with a tiny, pink-plastic sandwich sword. Steve started whooping with laughter immediately.

I frowned. "Um, Roland—" I started.

"Just *don't lose it,*" Roland said, immediately rolling up the grocery bag and turning his attention back to the maps. "And remember that the purpose is simple: to ensure that you are not lost in someone else's dreaming *permanently,* outside the Place of Solace."

Not wanting to advertise my *incredible* "talisman" any longer than necessary, I shoved it into my pants pocket. Even Julie was stifling laughter, and refused to meet my eyes for moments after.

Roland was rolling up the maps for us to take with us. Suddenly, the memory of the car ride with the monster hunters after Amanda's party came back to me. "Oh, my God!" I shouted. "That's right. They wanted to *kill* him!"

Everyone stopped and turned to me. "Who wanted to—" Julie started.

"Those *monster hunters*!" I said. "That's what they were trying to do! Kill Mike! Before—"

"Before *Pete* killed *them*," Julie finished.

Steve gasped. "Pete *killed* them?" he said. "Holy shit. Why the fuck didn't anyone tell me this?" He set his backpack down with a sigh. "*Now* who the fuck am I gonna buy grass from?"

ROLAND DIRECTED US TO a secret doorway that looked exactly like a wall between two other doors.

"Clever idea," I said. Roland beamed.

The door opened to reveal a finely cobbled city street by night, lit by gas lamps on either side. Their flickering lights illuminated darkened shop windows.

"My dreaming ends shortly after the bend in the lane," Roland said. "But I'm guessing the campus will be populated, based on what's in that journal. So you ought to be able to ask someone for directions."

As usual, Steve simply bustled through the door. "Sounds good, old man," Steve said.

Julie followed him through. "Are you sure that *all three* of us should go at once?" she asked, turning.

Roland nodded. "Much greater chance that I can home in on you—as long as you stick together! I probably could have done a much better job with Charley's return if that had been the case."

I patted Roland on the shoulder. "Thank you, Roland," I said. "I'm going to try to make this quick."

Roland chuckled. "Just do your best!" he said. "I have confidence in all of you!"

I FINALLY BECAME FULLY aware of the *magnificence* of the Place of Solace, the World Behind/Beneath/Between (or whatever), and I began to understand something with great clarity. Steve figured it out at almost precisely the same moment, and with his usual tact, he blurted it out.

"I'd be pretty fucking pissed off too if someone made me build all this cool shit, and then basically said, 'Thanks, dude. Oh, and by the way? Fuck you! Get in that hole and stay there!'"

Even Julie nodded. "No shit," she said. "I mean, I get it. Laban was like a super-duper magician guy, he knew how to control these demons and shit, but did he have to be such a fucker about it?"

I had to admit that I was not ambivalent about the matter, either.

"Yeah," I said, gazing at the next intricately carven set of statues adorning the lane. "It's not *Roland's* fault, though—"

"Hell, no," Steve said. "That guy rocks. He's only *here* because of Laban."

I noted the bend in the lane up ahead. As we approached, the bend turned sharply to the right, where we were met with a large iron gate set in an archway, spanning the width of the lane. An extremely obvious keyhole sat in the middle of the gate.

Beyond the gate, the lane opened up into a rather extensive lawn lit by more gas lamps. At the farthest edge of the lawn were stone steps leading up to the pillared front of a classic university building.

I took out the key. "Hope this works," I said.

Julie and Steve both watched intently as I inserted the key and twisted it. A cranking sound, a wheezing, the sound of gears shifting, and suddenly—

"Looks like we made it," Julie said.

We were on the other side of the gate.

"Where did the key go?" I asked.

Steve shrugged. "We're in," he said. "Now we've just got to find a secret fraternity party that's somewhere near a bar that we don't know the location of, and we're good to go!"

"If that party's even going on tonight," I said.

"Good point," Julie said. "But the *other* key should be there, one way or the other."

At the same moment, I noticed a few people milling about up ahead. Steve sprinted off toward them.

"He's ideal bait," Julie said. "Unthinking, perfectly willing."

"At this point, I have no problem with that," I said.

Steve was talking animatedly with two well-dressed young men moments later. Julie and I decided to hang back and let him work his dysfunctional magic on them.

We sat down on a bench near one of the lamps. I felt the little plastic sandwich sword in my pants pocket, and shifted until I could ignore it.

Steve appeared to be shaking hands with one of the guys. All three were laughing. Then one of them pulled out a pen and appeared to make a sketch on a sheet of paper.

"How does he *do* that?" I asked. Julie was shaking her head.

Moments later, Steve trotted back to us.

"Peace of *cake*, dudes!" he said, waving the sheet of paper in my face. "They thought it was some kind of test. They kept calling me 'Finnegan,' and I just kept denying it!"

I grabbed the flyer and looked at it. It was an unlabeled map with an X at the center, a curvy line leading past a few squares, and a star with a circle around it at the end of the line.

"Let me guess," I said. "That's us, at the X?"

Steve nodded. "Yep," he said, grabbing the paper back. "We should maybe stop at that party for a minute, you know, after getting the key—"

"Don't you think that was a little too, you know, *easy*?" Julie remarked.

I shrugged. "Easy or not, it's a lead," I said. "Let's just give it a shot."

That's a TERRIBLE idea!

The three of us immediately jolted. The voice came—*thunderingly* loud, in fact—but somehow quite obviously not "out there."

"You guys heard that—" I began.

Of COURSE they did! the thunder spoke. *Look at them! Shitting their pants—just like YOU!*

The internal rumbling faded. Julie spoke first. "Roland?" she said sheepishly.

Oh, how fucking TYPICAL! it pounded out. *You meet ONE Dreamkeeper and you think he's responsible for—*

"He *said* that he wasn't going to be *available* at this point," Steve said, wagging a finger at Julie. She glared at him.

Don't interrupt me!

Steve shut up.

Now—are you SURE you want to go through with this? the voice asked. *Getting that other key, I mean?*

We all looked at each other. A breeze had picked up, and there appeared to be something of a crowd gathering near the steps of the building up ahead.

Because, you COULD just stick around, you know, it continued. *Join them at the Midsummer Revelry! It's a blast. The Fairy Queen's super-cute. Maybe finish a degree? Or two? Easy enough to arrange. THOSE fuckers seem to be enjoying it.* Somehow we knew it was indicating the crowd of people that had gathered.

"Can I ask" —I hesitated, momentarily— "*who* you are?"

Certainly, it said without answering. *Now, I'm just going to warn you once more. THERE WILL BE BLOOD. Just imagine it. I'm talking BUCK-ETS of that shit! Like CARRIE-level shit, man!*

"Like *who*?" Steve asked.

Never mind, it responded. *All right. You want to play stupid? Fine.*

"*I* don't want to play stupid!" I insisted. Julie was nodding frantically.

Go ahead and get your little fucking key.

The voice went silent.

WE FOUND THE DOOR labeled "TRAP." Whatever the "Midsummer Revelry" was had kicked in by the time we got there—people were getting trashed by the truckload *fast*.

"What did I tell you guys?" Steve said. "Cake. Just cake."

Entering through it—

Yuletide 1936.

The Old Court
Providence, RI

My dear Laban,

This man Lovecraft turns out to be as surly and quite as ingenious as you indicated in your letter of the 4ᵗʰ. He has been worn down, at least; but whatever it is that the physicians are providing him with fails to loosen his tongue quite enough for our purposes. I fear that we do not have much time. When I saw him last (just two days ago), he appeared thin as a rail and white as a sheet.

Something eats away at him more thoroughly than the rot in his belly. I read what I could find of his work, but the bits and pieces are hardly enlightening. Trying to guess the location of the Carter property from the hints in the story is like trying to find one particular star in the night sky while wearing a blindfold! Even then, who's to say that the Snake Den isn't a relic or some indefinable mound of earth by this point?

The formulas he provided, however, were quite correct. There is nothing we can really do about that; sufficient obscurations were provided when he published them that he has broken no oaths of obligation.

We cannot at this time force his hand.

I have given him the V.S., with hopes that he will make use of it in time. I fear he is quite done with us all, and recommend that you return to Candleston for one last look.

Yr. Obt. Svt.,

C. F.

THE LETTER ENDED WITH a flourish and the curious sigil that Curwen Flowers used to ensure that it would be read by none other than its intended recipient. Laban Black eased himself back from a great antique desk before the library window of his estate in Golem Creek and gazed at the snowfall outside. Other than crackling of embers from the hearth and wheezing of icy winds through pores in the house's walls, there was silence.

He was old, and he was tired.

All the work that had been done, contracts forged and signed, agreements made, nights spent in suffering and pain and all the terrible agonies incumbent upon the One who was to return—would it all amount to nothing? A single Dreamer's decision to withhold the Key...

Laban rubbed his eyes.

To die with it all not only unfinished, but with the weight of Rumor holding his casket down, in infamy, his name tarnished, his family ruined.

He would leave it all to Curwen, of course. Curwen who had stayed loyal no matter what absurdities dogged Laban's every effort; Curwen Flowers, True Son of Yog Sothoth. He had no doubt in his mind that, if it could be done, even at this late hour, Curwen would find a way to do it.

There was a light knock at the library door behind him.

Laban took a breath, wincing slightly at a pain in his ribs. "Enter."

The door opened. "Your afternoon tea, sir," Miles said. "I'll set it here for you. Is there anything else you require, sir?"

Laban did not turn around. He wanted to laugh, but such effort was beyond him at this point. Anything else he required?

"No, Miles, thank you. That will be all," he said. He heard the door close quietly.

Outside, snow continued to fall, without any sign of stopping. Laban opened a drawer in the great old desk and extracted a sheet of yellowing paper.

My dear Curwen... he began.

SOMETHING TERRIBLY WRONG ABOUT the whole affair. Things should have been taken care of by now. A demonic intercession? No issue. Extractions of the essences from a few local ladies when the stars were right? Fine.

Get a blasted key from a dying man? Impossible!

Curwen sat cross-legged on the floor before a makeshift altar in his room at the Old Court and began his usual procedure. The mirror before him, twin black candles in sticks shaped like satyrs to either side, began to vibrate and hum with the *bijamantra* of the Old Ones. The familiar sensation, as if his mind somehow sloped to one side, announced a perichoresis of dimensions.

And a mauve light, through the Cone, in the midst of infinity, poured forth from the mirror into the room.

Waves of Great Bliss flooded through him. Even at this stage, Curwen struggled somewhat to retain a speck of individual awareness as oceans of Reality in all its forms threatened to overwhelm it—not "him," as he would have said in any other state of mind, only "it," that creature rising up out of the infinitude, known as Curwen Flowers to the droves of mortal men.

For these fools of men and their woes care not thou at all...

The words of the Book—or one of them, at least. Again, the struggle...that was not a struggle. "It cannot be attained by effort." The words of another Book—or was that a Man, perhaps?

And suddenly—silence. Ah, but there was the trick! The silence was a ruse. The Great Secret. The Abbé Constant had conferred this Truth to Laban directly, after visiting him in Golem Creek. "You are a man of inconstant fortunes"—the usual *vert langue* made use of, the old rogue!—"but I will give you a Treasure priceless beyond measure: you are silent, you are not silent, you are not-not silent..."

Two negations of a negative. And Yog Sothoth

is attained...

"THE THING ABOUT DREAMS is their outlandish overlap," Howard said at last. "One thing becomes another thing; indeed, it *is* that thing—both things at the same time! And yet, in consequence, neither."

Curwen sipped his coffee. Howard gazed longingly at the pot of it sitting on the little round table between them, but couldn't bring himself to indulge. Nothing worked inside him any longer; the consequences of any intermingling with the external world were now empirically—as they had always otherwise been—disastrous.

"What I have written of these things, Curwen, is thus no longer of consequence," he said.

Curwen took another sip of coffee, this time anxiously. "You're telling me that the Key no longer exists?" he said.

The hint of a smile played thinly over Howard's features. "You want to know if something I imagined no longer exists?" he responded.

Curwen set down his cup and sighed. "Blast it all, Howard!" he said. "You *brought* us here! You made it *so*! If anyone can empathize with us, it is *you.*"

The smile faded. "I'm sorry," Howard said, seeming genuinely apologetic. "Truly, I am. But Carter is gone. I cannot bring him back. *I cannot write his name any longer.*"

Curwen stood up from the table. A drizzling rain had begun outside. It would be a cold, wet walk back to the inn.

"Have you considered the Wine?" he asked, gazing out the little attic window.

Howard nodded. "Indeed I have," he answered. "But I can assure you that it won't do any good. Not now."

All that work... Curwen thought to himself. *And now—powerless in the face of our Creator—*

"There is one way," Howard said quietly.

Curwen breathed deeply and returned from the window. "We have *no idea* who or what it will engender," he said. "Future, past? Gone and done with! 'All are one in Him,'" Curwen quoted.

Howard pointed to a small stack of papers on a rickety wooden desk in the corner. "Take them," he said. "The others have already received a portion. Enough if they've got the brains to unravel it. What I've given you is—" he coughed into one pale hand, his face reddening. After a pause, he continued, almost silently. "Enough."

Curwen scooped up the small stack of pages from the desk and walked briskly to the door. He turned the door handle and opened it.

"This is good-bye, then," he said.

Behind him, there was no response.

Curwen stepped out of the room and closed the door.

DESPITE PROTESTATIONS, AT LABAN'S calm and unprovoked insistence, Miles departed alone for Cornwall a week later. It was Laban's concern for the safety of the various items being sent along that finally convinced him, and the promise that Curwen was to return from Providence shortly, the latter with the ostensible aim of aiding Laban in his return journey, back home, back to Wales.

Miles had sensed the lies at the outset, of course, but what recourse did he have?

The house was in order, the necessary papers drawn up, leaving the estate in its entirety to Curwen, with instruction to send along sufficient means for Miles to retire and live out his days in some degree of comfort, after decades of loyal service.

In the quiet, in the cold, Laban dressed himself in ritual garments, speaking the words of consecration as he did so. A familiar sensation suddenly warmed him. Always, like an artist or musician, once clothed in ritual finery, Laban no longer felt the pains and vicissitudes of age upon him.

Laban spoke the combination of words that opened a hidden door into the sub-basement of his mansion and descended a set of stone steps into the Chamber. Fires sprang up at his command in sconces set into walls of dark granite. He hefted the small brazier to the right of the entrance, a fog of lignum aloes and frankincense and all necessary suffumigations spilling forth.

"I burn this in the Name and to the Honor of Yog Sothoth," he spoke, and entered the Circle, one final time.

—was just as easy as we initially thought.

I stepped back out of the door brandishing the key, which looked nearly identical to the previous one, if a bit more tarnished. It also had a little tag tied to one end of it with thread, like you'd find at an antique store. "HPL/RC" was penned neatly on it in brownish ink.

"That was..." I trailed off. I noticed that my right eye felt tender to the touch.

"Super easy," Julie said.

"Yeah, no shit," Steve added.

"Okay," I said. "Not the worst thing in the world."

"So," Julie said. "I kind of expected something horrible to happen. Or *something*." She took a closer look at me. "Did you hurt yourself?"

"Kind of expected *something*," Steve said, walking ahead of us. "Like getting attacked, maybe. Or one of us dying."

"I guess," I said, touching my eye lightly again. "Let's be thankful. That nothing happened. Right?"

We started back to the gate. The Revelry was in full swing. People were literally hanging out of windows and in the branches of trees, acting like complete animals. At one point, I could have *sworn* that I saw a girl that looked almost *exactly* like Molly in the midst of one crowd in the distance, wearing a glimmering tiara. Someone was fanning her with a huge swathe of peacock feathers.

I lost track of her when a troop of half-naked students swooped into our midst from out of nowhere, banging on drums and shouting and screaming like maniacs. I kept glancing at the key, and wondering. I recalled—well, I *didn't* so much recall actually *getting* it. But then again, I kind of did.

I kept wanting to just forget about it and move on. Julie, and especially Steve, seemed unnaturally silent about it as well.

GREAT JOB! THE THUNDER-VOICE rolled in as we approached the gate. *Wow! Okay, I guess I underestimated you guys.*

"Yeah, well," I said.

"Yeah, dude!" Steve said, suddenly regaining his nerve. "You bet your *ass* you did."

Ass officially handed over, it answered.

"Damn straight," Steve replied.

I suppose I owe you all a sincere apology, it said, with the distinct aura of a chuckle behind its "words." *But in lieu of that, how about I just let you go—back to that little prissy Roland's "safe place."*

A *huge* wind kicked up, propelling us to the iron gate—

—and through, into the silence of the gas-lit street at the edge of the Place of Solace.

"Hell, *yeah!*" Steve exclaimed. "Objective one: *accomplished.* Killed *that* sonofabitch! Woo-hoo!"

He skipped on ahead of me and Julie.

In the distance, partially illuminated once more by the wicked circle of the moon above, stood the pyramid of Laban Black, waiting, seeming preter-naturally calm in the instantaneous and jarring silence.

I tried to shrug off the worry that gnawed at me.

"Getting nervous?" Julie asked.

I shrugged. "If by that you mean 'still incredibly fucking nervous,' then, yeah, I am."

GETTING TO THE PYRAMID: easy and fun. Getting *into* the pyramid? A motherfucker.

The lovely and intricate setup of the Place of Solace, with the rather awe-inspiring and beautiful edifice of Laban's pyramid forming the backdrop and goal ahead of us, made the half-day trip through winding streets and shop corners, neighborhoods and sculpted forests, a much-needed source of relaxation. The steps leading up to the entrance of the pyramid, however, were nasty, brutish, and tall.

"Did he get *giants* to build these fucking stairs?" Steve asked as we performed the half-leaping maneuver necessary to get from one step up to the next.

I didn't have the breath to answer him. Julie was winded after every third step or so. "You guys go on ahead," she said at several points. In each case, our response was to sit down and take a breather.

The only good thing to come out of our forced inattention to the matter at hand was the view.

It was magnificent.

The billion details Laban had incorporated into the city were evident. At each observation made by either me or Steve, Julie simply nodded her head in acknowledgment.

Halfway up the pyramid we finally reached a landing and a heavy wooden door, in the center of which was an ornate lock in the shape of an imp's face. Its mouth formed the keyhole.

We paused to rest. I noticed what appeared to be a *coastline* many leagues off in the distance.

"That kind of freaks me out," Julie said.

"No shit," Steve observed. "Think about it. Like

when you go off-screen in a video game."

"You just keep on going," I said. "Forever."

"We still need to *investigate* this place!" Steve insisted. "I wish we could have gotten permission from Roland to fuck some shit up."

"Why do we need permission from Roland?" Julie said. "Oh, God. Did I just *encourage* you?"

"I don't need encouragement," Steve said. "Just liquor and ladies!"

"That would technically be encouragement," I had to say.

"Then I guess I can't live without encouragement!" Steve concluded.

"You're right, though," I said. "All this *stuff...* just *sitting* here."

"Yeah," Julie said. "Jackpot."

"It's weird, though," I said. "I mean, I could hang out here the rest of my life. Probably wouldn't ever find the end of all of this." I waved a hand at the coastline. "But if I knew I couldn't get back to Golem Creek at all, *ever...*"

"It'd be like prison," Julie said.

Steve snorted. "Fuck *that*," he said. "Do they have Johnny Walker Blue for breakfast in *prison*?"

"That's not what I mean," I said.

"Well, *whatever* you mean, I want you to know, right now, one thing," Steve said.

"What's that?" I asked

"You're *wrong*," he answered. "A jackpot's a jackpot. Just like food to a starving person is still just food—but if they *throw it away*, and don't *eat* it, then that person's just a fucking *idiot*."

Julie brightened up. "I think that was actual wisdom, Steve," she said, chuckling.

"Fuck yeah it was," he said.

I gazed back at the coastline, the ridge of mountainous structures against the horizon, the extraordinary *wealth* of the Place of Solace. I stood up and got out the key.

I noticed that I was, quite inadvertently, smiling.

I REMEMBERED THIS SENSATION: *down, down, down, into darkness.*

After unlocking the heavy wooden door with the key, I pushed it open, then extracted the key and peered inside. More stairs—this time leading down at a decently sloping angle to an indiscernible darkness. Lit torches appeared regularly on the walls to either side, but these only served to emphasize repetitive landings, and the closeness of the staircase seemed somewhat more oppressive given the sheer expansiveness we had admired mere moments before.

"After you," Steve said, waving a hand in the direction of the staircase. I gave him a sarcastic grin, and entered.

We descended. I found myself dizzy and winded in short order.

Again, we took regular pauses. Occasionally, Steve or Julie would get up before me and take the lead; then one or the other of us would switch places.

When we had been descending for some time, I began to feel it: *pressure.*

"Do you guys feel that?" I asked.

"Like we're in an airplane going *down*," Julie said. "How much farther is it to—well, to whatever we're supposed to find?"

"'Not far now,'" Steve said. I heard him chuckling.

"Please no Papa Smurf references," Julie said.

"Just trying to lighten the mood," Steve said. "You know, we probably should have thought to bring a garbage can lid with us."

"For what?" I asked. "A shield?"

"No, dude!" Steve said. "Stair-sledding! We'd basically already be there."

"True enough," Julie said. "Like the last time you did that. Remember? Maple Ridge?"

"Oh, *yeah!*" Steve said. "That was awesome!"

"That was a broken wrist, sprained ankle, and four stitches," Julie reminded him.

"Like I said!" Steve responded.

"It's a miracle," I said. "Check it out!"

We had entered a large stone room, again lit with torches, at the bottom of the stairs. Three shimmering pools of what I can only describe as *radiant blackness* swam before us, apparently three different exits from the room.

I groaned. "This is not what I need right now," I said. "Portals?"

"Choose *wisely*, Indy!" Steve said.

"Cut the crap, Steve," Julie said. "Seriously, how are we supposed to know which one to choose?"

Steve had stepped up close to one of them. "We're in a room," he said. "No windows..."

"Will you *please* stop quoting movies and help out!" Julie said.

"I *am* helping," Steve said. "This is how I think."

Julie made an exasperated noise. Then she noticed my obvious hesitation as I looked from one portal to the next repeatedly.

"You're not thinking—" she started.

"That's *exactly* what I'm thinking," I said. "And I *hate* the idea."

"You want each of us to take a different one?" Steve said.

"I don't *want* each of us to—" I said.

"Sure thing, dude," Steve said. "See you on the other side!"

He stepped through the left-hand portal and disappeared.

"Ah!" Julie exclaimed. "What is *wrong* with him?"

"He kind of just made our decision for us," I said.

"No," Julie said. "We could both just follow him."

"But is that the best idea?" I said. "What if that's the path with the monster, or whatever?"

"I kind of don't care," Julie answered. "Don't we have a better chance with three people?"

I shook my head. "*Here*?" I said. "I don't think numbers has much to do with it."

"Except that we have three portals," she said. "Please don't walk through a different one."

I hesitated. "I think it's our best bet, Julie," I said. "You can follow me if you want. We'll still increase our odds of figuring something out by taking a different path than Steve."

I began to step through the middle portal.

"Wait—" I heard, before blackness.

I AWOKE TO THE sound of William Shatner's voice in Pete Jarry's den.

He was sitting in another bean bag chair in front of the TV set, watching *Star Trek* and eating Cap'n Crunch. I noticed that it was the "all crunchberries" kind.

I sat up from a pile of cushions and groaned.

"You awake?" Pete said. "Man, you've been asleep for like two days!"

"No, Pete," I said. "I haven't. This is a dream, or some kind of test, or a diversion of some sort."

He raised his eyebrows at me.

"I took the wrong portal," I said.

He nodded knowingly. "Tell me about it," he said, turning back to the TV. Spock was in earnest, attempting to convey something of grave importance to Kirk. "I've done *that* before. More than once."

I stood up. My backpack was present, and I checked it for contents. There was the key, rations, water bottle... I checked my pockets. The pink sandwich-sword—still there. I shoved it unceremoniously back and tried to forget about it.

I figured I might as well play along and hope that things started to make sense.

"So, Pete," I said, diving in. "When did you start turning into a demon?"

Pete looked up at me seriously. "I wish you wouldn't remind me of that," he said. He set down his bowl of crunchberries.

"Well, too late," I said, starting to feel super-frustrated. "You're reminded. Explain yourself!"

"It's not me—" he began.

"Oh, the classic werewolf cop-out!" I yelled at him. "Honestly, Pete, don't you think that you should take *some* responsibility for—"

"No! I'm serious!" he said. "It's not *me!*" He looked thoughtful for a moment. "And I don't think it's a werewolf. I mean, I got this stuff—"

"Stuff?" I said. Now I was confused.

"Yeah!" Pete continued. "I got this stuff from a guy, a couple years ago. He wasn't my usual supplier. He said if I wanted to get high—like *really*, super-insanely high—that I *needed* to try this stuff."

Pete got up and walked over to the Easter Island head. He pressed a latch on the back of it, and the head opened to reveal a secret compartment.

"I should have known," I said.

"So, I was like, 'Sure, dude, as long as it's not crack or something.' And the guy laughs and says, 'No way! I only sell sweet-catch trips not wrestling-match trips.' And I always remembered that, because I still don't know what it means." He lifted an Altoids tin out of the head. "Anyway, I get home and I try some of it out, you know? And— *woah!* I was, like, in this other guy's head—but it wasn't a guy. It was like a monster—and I know because I could kind of *control* what he was doing, a little bit. And I started getting pretty good at it."

He opened the tin and showed me what appeared to be some candy Valentine's Day hearts, the kind with words printed on them. Except in addition to "BE MINE" and "I LOVE YOU," these had strange figures scrawled on one side. I couldn't discern what any of the latter meant.

"Check it out," he said, pointing at them. "So I kept taking these, maybe once a week. All sorts of wild shit happened. Sometimes I would just be able to see what was going on in other places—like I didn't have a body. That was useful, sometimes. I found myself in this underground world once. I could speak this weird language, and I could understand it, but it wasn't English, that's for sure. And one day, I found this exit, and I climbed up and out of it." Pete snapped shut the tin, put it in his bathrobe pocket, and sat down in his usual red-and-white bean bag chair. "And it was the *Murk*, man! But whoever's head I was in, he started gettin' real creepy—I wasn't really able to control it once I was out of that well."

Pete miraculously produced a dimebag of weed and started loading one of his bongs. "And then I started going into trances—like, without taking the stuff. In the middle of the day, sometimes— just fading off into these weird dreams. Something would trigger it—usually it was a song or a word that someone would say. Totally creeped me out. This thing wanted to rip people apart, and kept letting me know about it." He shuddered and took a hit. His pothead instincts had him offer the bong to me, but I shook my head.

The question of why the gentle druggie had seemingly indulged in wanton, cold-blooded murder had been answered to my satisfaction, even if it raised even *more* questions about what was going on in the underworld of Golem Creek.

"Pete," I said. "You're all right, man. But you need to get rid of that stuff, I think."

His eyes glazed over. "No shit, dude," he said. "High fructose *bullshit*, man."

THE NOTION THAT THERE was someone out there in Golem Creek selling monster-trance drugs made my skin crawl. If those sigils in the well had been placed intentionally by the Monster Squad in order to keep the demons from getting to the surface, then someone seemed to have found a way around it—human souls, maybe, acting as a way to bypass the supernatural alarms?

I was just guessing, of course, but it wasn't comforting either way.

Someone started banging on the doors leading to the basement from outside.

Pete seemed oblivious. "Could you get that for me, dude?" he asked. "I don't know about standing up right now." He laughed briefly.

I headed up the stairs. Daylight crept through the seam between the doors, which I unlatched and threw open.

A man stood there nervously, dark hair, dark eyes, glasses. He was dressed simply in jeans, T-shirt, and black hoodie. I suddenly recognized some of Pete's features—

"Stek!" I shouted.

He winced and put a finger to his lips. "*Sh!*
Keep your voice down!" he said. "Come on. Let's
go get what you came for."

"How did you—" I started.

"Never mind," he said. "This is portal business.
I'm in up to my goddamned neck, and we've got
to make sure that your little prom queen doesn't
get anywhere *near* that one down in the Murk."

He started off toward the street. "Hang on, one
second!" I whispered harshly. He stopped and stood
there, looking at me expectantly. "Let me just grab
my stuff!"

I ran back down the stairs.

"Is that Stek?" Pete asked. "Dude! Tell him to
come on down—"

"Uh, maybe some other time," I said nervously.
"I think he's in a hurry."

Pete nodded. "Ten-four, dude," he said. "You
guys should totally come back over, though, later.
I got that new VHS—"

"Totally," I said, running back up the stairs
with my backpack. I shut the doors behind me.

Stek was waiting impatiently across the street.

"Stek, you've *got* to be more clear with me,"
I said, jogging up to him. "I just came through
Laban Black's tomb—"

"Yeah, I *know*," he said. "And you were the
only one with the Silver Key. So your two friends
might be as good as *dead.*"

I suddenly felt phenomenally stupid and terribly guilty. Julie...and Steve, of course. But Steve
damned himself! Julie had tried to stop me...

"How the hell were we supposed to know which portal to take?" I said.

"It was a failsafe mechanism!" Stek said. "Whoever holds the key can take *any one* of them and be all right. But without the key, you just end up—" Stek interrupted himself. "Don't worry about that right now."

"So why am *I* here, then?" I asked. He had started along a path between two houses. "I've got the key. Why aren't I in Laban's tomb, or whatever?"

"You are," he said, not turning around. "Please note that I am not looking at you. But I am aware, nonetheless, of the look on your face."

"I get it," I said. "Being surprised at this point would be like being surprised that kicking a soccer ball makes it move."

"Basically," he said. "I want to get out of here as much as—no, *more than*—you do. I got stuck here after I made the mistake of trying to figure out what the hell was going on in Golem Creek. That wasn't very long ago—*your* time."

"So where are we going again?" I said.

"Hey, I'll tell you what," he said. "You just follow along, do what I tell you *when* I tell you, and I'll explain everything later. Okay? Does that sound fair?" He immediately began walking away again.

I could sense his annoyance, but I wasn't about to be brushed off.

"No," I said. I stopped walking. "I'm done with this mysterious bullshit. Where are my friends?"

Stek started smiling as he turned back around.

"Would it make you feel better if I just told you they're dead?"

I looked him directly in the eyes. "No," I said. "Are they?"

"Let's go ask the Fairy Queen," he said.

WE HAD TAKEN THE back way to Molly Furnival's house.

"Okay," he said. "I'll let you go around front and knock."

"Wait," I said. "*Molly*?"

Stek nodded. "Who better, right? Who did you think that creature at Amanda's party was trying to capture and carry off, anyway?"

"Not *Molly*," I admitted. "And how the hell would *you* know that? Has that party even *happened* yet in this timeline?"

"Oops," he said. "Forget I said anything. Just go see if you can get her to take a walk with you down to the Murk."

"Creepy, a little," I said.

"No way, man," Stek said. "Classic."

"Then what?" I asked.

"Have her try a sip of this." Stek handed me a miniature flask.

"Oh, Christ, Stek," I responded, holding the flask in front of me like a dead fish. "You want me to *rufie* her?"

"*Elf*-rufie, man!" Stek objected strenuously. "Or fairy. Whatever." He waved to the house. "Go, already."

I held out the flask to him. "I am morally incapable of this," I said. "Besides, she's not going to drink it."

Stek hesitated. "Fine," he said. "It'll be a last resort. Just keep her busy, then, for about twenty or thirty minutes. But if she starts acting all crazy, like she *really* needs to get back to the house, you *must* make her drink that. Throw it at her if you have to."

"Why?" I demanded.

"Because her parents—or those two mortals she's co-opted into *being* her parents—are both at their normal, boring jobs right now," he said. "And I have to break in and rob them."

STEK REFUSED TO SPEAK further on the matter. "I'll *explain* everything *later*, man," he promised. "Just *keep her busy*. And like I said, *do not let her return to the house* until you get my signal."

I shoved the flask into a side pocket on my backpack, resigning myself to the situation. "Whatever, man," I said. "What's the signal?"

"I'll make it obvious, whatever it is," he said, "but I'll have to improvise based on how the burglary goes. Now hurry up!"

He literally shoved me toward the house. I turned and trudged around the side, noting the neatly trimmed shrubbery that lined one edge of her property. I could see the windows of her house up above. Perhaps...*that* one was her room? Light-pink drapes, some books, page-edges out, facing the glass. The house was built into the ascending curve where Willow Street turned into Cresthill. She literally awoke to a view of her entire neighborhood, and part of the forest beyond, sprawling beneath her.

Like a queen and her kingdom, I thought. I had moved beyond the point of questioning things much further—Molly, some type of Fairy Queen? Of course, it seemed perfectly possible—to *me*, like storybook stuff, but—

"See anything you like, Charley?"

It was Molly. At her *mailbox.* Gazing back at me, as I gazed up into her bedroom window.

"Ah!" I exclaimed. *Think fast, man!* "Molly! I'm *so* glad to run into you! I was just taking a walk—"

"Through my *backyard?*" she said. I noticed that she was grinning, at least. That had to mean something.

I stopped moving. This would have to be good.

"Yes, Molly, that's correct," I said. "I figured the best way to ask you out on a real date would be to skulk like some kind of weirdo through your backyard. Maybe leave terribly ambiguous messages written in ketchup on your back porch. Like: 'See you around, babe.' That would be a good one to start out with."

Molly's grin widened into a smile, then laughter. "I'm eager to read your work, Charles," she said. "In the meantime, I was about to walk down to Tanya's. We're going to Amanda Whitfield's party. You want to tag along?"

Amanda Whitfield's...?

Sure, why not. Head to the party three times in one night. Never thought to ask Pete what god-damned day it was. I should have known that I'd slip back in time *again.* What was it about Amanda

Whitfield's party? Was every goddamned portal in town geared to bring me back to that fucking party?

The point was to keep her away from the house, which she was leaving anyway. Thanks, Stek. At least maybe this time I could be positively sure Molly didn't get eaten by a demon...*which was going to be partially possessed by Pete Jarry...*

"Absolutely," I said, trying to hide my rising anxiety. If I had perfect timing—*perfect* timing—I might be able to kill two birds with one stone. Or, rather, *not* kill them.

Molly held out her hand to me. "Come on! Have you seen the view from the top of Cresthill?"

IT WAS *GLORIOUS*. I needed no sun, and all lights paled, mere imitations of her radiance. I could barely contain effusions of adoration, except for silence in favor of her voice, even her footsteps, which sounded like orchestrations beautifying the trees, the flowers, the—

Had I fallen asleep?

The sun had set. Moonlight glinted off the tops of trees visible on Chicken Hill across the valley of Golem Creek. I awoke with a start, and could barely eliminate the absurd smile plastered on my face, even as rampant anxiety kicked in.

I was supposed to keep her from going back home—

I sat up straight. I lay in a little copse of trees at the top of Cresthill Drive, which I could see down a slope just in front of me. I could also smell wood burning, and as I stood up, I noticed flashing lights and flickering tongues of flame arising some distance off.

Molly's house.

By the time I got to the end of Cresthill, what with firetrucks and a thronging chaos of people, I knew there wasn't much of a chance that either my mission here—whatever the hell that was—*or* Molly's comfortable little bedroom had survived.

I detoured and headed back to Pete's.

"HE DIDN'T HAVE TO *burn the place down*!" In a harsh whisper, I confronted Pete, who had somehow made it onto his roof. He stared in the direction of the smoking remains of Molly's house, entranced.

"No *shit*, right?" he answered. Pete proceeded to descend from the roof via a half-concealed ladder leaning against it to one side.

"Where the hell is Stek?" I demanded. "I mean, did he get what he needed, or what?"

I followed Pete around the side of his house back to the basement doors, where he waved me into the basement proper, then closed the doors behind us. Stek sat on the floor of the basement with what appeared to be a miniature distillation train laid out before him.

"I *got* it!" he exclaimed, standing up as Pete and I entered the room.

"Got *what*, exactly?" I asked, gazing at a fluid—dark, yet somehow iridescent, like motor oil in sunlight—piping through a condenser tube into a flask.

"The *stuff*, man! The Witch's Wine!" Stek said, waving a hand toward the setup on the floor. The

Bunsen burner beneath a boiling flask at one end seemed to flare up a bit at that moment, as if waving at us. Pete sauntered off to the inner stairs and up to the house proper, typically unfazed.

Despite its appearance, the "stuff" gave off an odor reminiscent of cake frosting or Pixie Stick dust. "That's wonderful, Stek," I said, unsure of what it was or why he needed it. "But was it *absolutely necessary* to burn down Molly's house to *get* it, man? And speaking of which: *where the hell* is *she, anyway*?"

Stek was shaking his head, and had returned to his position, seated cross-legged on the floor, attending to each drip and drop of the Witch's Wine. "That was *her* decision, dude," he said. "*I* didn't burn the place down. *She* did. Which wouldn't have happened, of course, if you had done your fucking job."

I was taken aback. "*My* job? What the hell do you mean?"

"You were *supposed* to keep her *away from the house* while I was in there," he responded. "I give you the benefit of the doubt, however. It's not like you have any practice in dealing with the fascinations and glamors of Fairy Queens." Stek shook his head. "Which doesn't really matter now, does it, since we *got the stuff*!"

"*She* burnt down the house?" I repeated, ignoring most of everything he had said.

Stek nodded and gazed back up at me, retrieving a bent box of Marlboros from his shirt pocket. "Mm-hm," he confirmed. "She totally flipped out. Eyes flaming and all that. Her attempt to kill me resulted in some bad-assery on my part," he smiled broadly, "and her failure to either do so *or* stop me from getting the stuff."

"So Molly Furnival, the Fairy Queen, was hiding this magic potion in the house she shared with two unwitting mortals," I summarized. "Can you maybe tell me, Stek, why we couldn't just *ask* her for the damned stuff?"

Stek shook his head. "No way," he answered. "First of all, fairies? They don't give shit away. It would have cost like a billion dollars or my soul or something like that. Second, the whole point is to keep shit like this from people like us."

"Maybe she'd understand if we explained it to her?" I suggested.

"No fucking way!" Stek insisted. "She already *knows* what this could be used for. Mortals? We're just fucking nuisances. As far as most magical creatures are concerned, the job of humans is to fuck shit up and then beg for help—from *them*, mind you—when the obvious happens." Stek sighed. "I totally get why you think we should have done it 'the easy way,' but I assure you: in the end, you and I are still humans. And to *them*, that just doesn't count."

Stek's answer bothered me for numerous reasons. He was probably right; probably most of what I felt for Molly was just the effects of fairy dust. But I wasn't ready to *believe* that yet.

I left it alone for the time being. I certainly didn't believe I would convince Stek of anything. He seemed pretty single-minded.

"Where is she now?" I asked. I was reasonably

sure I knew the answer to that question, but the timeline had already altered at least once so far. I wouldn't be surprised if it changed again.

"Let's just say I took care of her." Stek grinned. He lit one of his bent cigarettes.

"How so?" I asked.

"With this." He retrieved a handgun from beneath a pillow beside him.

"Jesus *Christ*, Stek!" I shouted. "You *killed* her?"

Stek gave me a look of terrific displeasure. "As *if*, man!" he said. "No, I didn't *kill* her. I don't even know how that would be done. But I *did* probably put her in something of a bind for a little while."

The potion sputtered in the setup as all of the contents from one end of the distillation train finally spat out into the flask at the other end.

"Straight answer, please?" I pleaded.

Stek retracted the Bunsen burner wick and lifted the flask, shaking it gently and gazing at it in the dim light. "The bullets in this gun were forged in the fires of Mount Doom," he began.

My eyes must have been goggling. Stek started cracking up.

"Just kidding, dude!" he said. "I merely debilitated her. I think. I've never used these bullets before on anything. Dead shot, though, man—six rounds right in the chest. She basically turned into a ball of fire and rocketed off." Stek laughed. "Through the roof, mind you. Which didn't help the arson going on downstairs!"

"Won't the *cops* be looking for you?" I pointed out.

"Absolutely," he said. "And they won't find me. Or you, for that matter. Because we're heading back to wake up ol' Laban and finish this mess. But first we're going to locate your friends. Like I *promised* I would." He turned his head toward the inner stairs. "Pete!" he shouted. "Get your ass down here! And bring me a Coke while you're at it!"

THE "STUFF" WAS CALLED *vinum sabbati,* which did not translate to "Witch's Wine," but Stek said that he preferred that phrase to "Wine of the Sabbath." Molly had "generated" this particular batch during the last Super Blood Blue Wolf Moon when three of the seven constellations of magical stars utterly invisible to mundane astronomers had entered the appropriate constellations in "Fairy Space."

Pete had returned with three overstuffed sandwiches and three Cherry Cokes, which we painstakingly devoured as Stek relayed this nonsense to me.

Despite my circumstances, I told Stek the truth.

"I don't believe a fucking *word* of this," I said.

Stek shrugged. "Suit yourself," he said. "At any rate, we've got to get this stuff to the Other Side ASAP." He chugged the rest of his Coke.

"Wait a second!" I said. "How does this help us locate Steve and Julie? I thought that's what we're supposed to do next."

"Hey, chill, man," Stek said. "We've got it under control. The most important part is done. Had to get some food in before Phase Two."

"What's Phase Two?" I asked, irritated.

"Pete, whenever you're ready," Stek said.

Pete smiled. "Rock 'n' roll, dude." He extracted the Altoids tin from his bathrobe pocket.

"Wait a second," I said. "You're going to trance out on *those*? That's a *terrible* idea!" Visions of monster hunters carrying a body bag out of Amanda Whitfield's house paraded through my mind. "Don't you realize—"

"I think I got a handle on it, man," Pete said, nodding and flipping open the tin. He gazed carefully at the candy Valentine's Day hearts inside. "Best bet for finding your friends. Stek knows what he's doing."

Stek nodded enthusiastically. "We used it to find Obi-Wan when he ran off two months ago," he said.

"Who the fuck is Obi-Wan?" I asked. Stek and Pete both looked at me, eyebrows raised, then burst into laughter after a beat.

"My mom's dachshund," Stek said. "Little fucker made it halfway across the *county*! Can you believe it?"

Pete sorted through the candies with one finger. "Let's see. '2 Hot 2 Handle.' I feel good about that one!"

Stek nodded at him. "Let's try and get our asses in gear, all right?" he said. "I'd like to make it to Max Plunkett's before sunrise. This is probably gonna suck."

I barely had a chance to respond to Stek's pronouncement of imminent death—or at least bullet wounds— before Pete was dissolving the candy heart under his tongue.

"Okay, Pete?" Stek inquired. Pete closed his eyes, leaning back restfully in his bean bag chair. "Now, we want to know: *where are Steve and Julie?*"

Pete's breathing had slowed substantially. I noticed a degree of perspiration on his forehead. His head slumped forward.

"He's going to be like this for a while," Stek said. "This happens every time. Want to watch TV?"

I shook my head. "No," I said, "not particularly."

After thirty minutes of Stek flipping through comic books at random, I almost gave in and turned the TV on. At that moment, Pete's head lifted up slowly. He began to half whisper and half mumble.

Stek dropped the copy of *Amazing Spider-Man* that he was reading and glanced at me. "Here we go," he said. We both sat there, looking at Pete as if he was the answer to the deepest secrets of the universe—which, in a sense, he kind of was.

Finally, I heard something more coherent. Pete spoke in a harsh whisper.

"*It's Pete! Pete Jarry! Don't shoot! I can control it!*"

Then silence. I recognized what he was saying instantly.

"Holy shit!" I said. "I think he's at Amanda Whitfield's party!"

"Pete?" Stek looked concerned. "Pete? Where are you?" He reached out and touched Pete gently on the shoulder. "Petey? Shit."

"What happened?" I asked.

"I think he's trying to regain control of it," Stek said. "The last time we tried this, the same thing happened. It's like whatever he gets inside of doesn't notice at first, and then when it does, it kicks him out. We'll just have to wait it out. Cigarette?"

I shook my head. "I'm sure he's at Amanda's," I said. "And if he *is*, then I know what just happened. But that's not the answer to the question we need." I realized what a bind we were in. Steve and Julie were at the party—sure. But I also knew *exactly* what happened after that...all the way up to *this very moment.*

I suddenly saw how clever Laban's "failsafe" mechanism was. If you chose the wrong portal, you had to go through everything *again* in order to get *back* to the point where you even had a *chance* to choose the right one. And who knew whether the location of the *right* portal changed in the meantime?

I began to feel drained. This was clearly not the solution to the puzzle. We both sat there, and the adrenaline from Pete's sudden awakening still powered Stek's attention. Pete did indeed appear to be struggling with something internally, twitching and grimacing occasionally, like he was having a bad dream.

Suddenly, he spoke again.

"Dudes! Dudes? Hey! Oh, man, this sucks."

I glanced over at Stek, who continued to gaze intently at Pete. "There's nothing we can do," I said.

"What?" Stek said. "Pete: where are you?"

"*Trunk of a car? I guess. Dark in here.*"

I had an idea. "Can you communicate with them, Pete?" I said.

"*Yo! Out there! Hey, it's Pete. Is anybody out there?*"

"Pete! Don't let them open it!" I shouted at him.

"*Go for it, man,*" Pete mumbled. "*Wait—what was that?*"

Pete raised his head and seemed to be trying to open his eyes. I slumped. "Those guys are dead," I said to Stek. "Son of a bitch."

Stek was trying to shake Pete awake.

"Is that a good idea?" I asked.

"I don't know!" Stek said. "It looks like he's having some kind of fit."

Pete collapsed back into the bean bag chair. Seconds later, he was snoring.

"Okay," I said. "Well, at least I know where Pete *was.*"

"Where, again?" Stek asked.

"A little ways from the Lots-a-Burger downtown," I answered. "But those monster hunter guys are *toast—*"

"Monster hunters?" he said. "You mean Booker and the gang? I sincerely doubt that. Grab your shit, man." He took the flask of Witch's Wine and stoppered it carefully with black plastic. "Let's go get a burger!"

"What about him?" I asked, wondering how in the world Stek would manage one more bite of food on top of the trencher he had just consumed.

"He'll be fine," Stek said as he wrapped the flask in newspaper and shoved it into a backpack. "He's got plenty of stuff here to take care of the hangover he'll have when he wakes up."

WE MADE IT OVER to the Lots-a-Burger in Stek's brown Camaro. The stench of the car's ashtray, overflowing with cigarette butts, gradually intermingled with that of fries and burgers piped into the air by the enterprising owner of Golem Creek's finest fast food establishment.

I continued to express my doubts about "Booker and the gang" to Stek during our drive as clearly as I could, all the while realizing that we had just missed me$_3$ and Julie at this very establishment. By this point, the two Julies, Steve, and me$_2$ had ended up back at the Dreamkeeper's Emporium after returning to the Brake Street house.

And if the deepest level of chaotic shit had been reached, then me$_1$, Julie, and Steve were now at Pete's for the "first" time this evening, having the finest dinner imaginable.

I tried to stick to my immediate context of problems without indulging too many whims about the novelty of it. I felt reasonably certain that of all people, Pete could handle it.

"I think those guys were killed by the monster that Pete was trying to control," I told him.

Stek snorted and fiddled with the radio dial. Guns N' Roses emerged from the static with "Mr. Brownstone." "Maybe *one* of them," he said. "But *all* of them? Those guys know what they're doing. They've dealt with worse."

Unsurprisingly, as we pulled into the Lots-a-Burger, I *heard* Steve well before I saw him.

"...that guy doesn't even know how to roll a *car*, much less a *joint!*" he said to laughter. "I mean, come *on!* Perfectly good, primo shit, right out the fucking window!"

We pulled up to a spot in the crowded parking lot two cars away. I saw now that Steve sat on the hood of the monster-hunters' Pontiac 6000 alongside the Lots-a-Burger, surrounded by crushed bags of fast food and plastic soda cups. Booker and Barton leaned against the wall under a fluorescent light, chuckling and smoking. Steve took a bite of a gigantic hot dog without pausing in his speech.

"You know what I mean? So you've got this chick, who ain't gonna be high any time soon, and this guy who's just failed his test in basic Weed Mechanics, and what does she do?"

"What does she do?" Booker asked.

Steve smiled and finished his hot dog. "She reaches into his pants," he said between chews, "and pulls out his *wallet* and takes out two *twenties.* 'That oughta cover it,' she says, and she gets out of the car and *walks the fuck home.*"

Booker and Barton were exploding with laughter as Stek and I approached.

"Stek!" Booker leaped at Stek and gave him a bear hug.

Steve's eyes bulged when he saw me. Smiling broadly, he dropped the tin foil wrapping of his hot dog on the ground. "Holy *shit,* man!" he exclaimed, hopping off the car. "Chaz the Great and Terrible! We were on our way to *find* you dude! Where the fuck you *been*?" He took a cue from Booker and hugged me. I returned the gesture weakly.

"What are you doing with these guys?" I whispered. "They're *dead*, Steve!"

We broke apart. Steve gave me a brief look of bewilderment. I feigned a smile. "You could have waited for us, you know," I said.

"I know, I know," he produced a cigarette and lit it, his eyes still indicating that he was trying to figure out what I had meant by my comment. "I'm sorry. Loose cannon. Hey, where's Jules? We got *work* to do, man!"

"You don't know?" I asked.

Steve shoved his Bic lighter back in his pocket. "No," he said slowly. "Please don't tell me I'm supposed to."

I ran a hand through my hair. "Steve," I said, shaking my head. "Shit."

Stek and the two monster hunters were conversing animatedly beside us. I noticed the two remaining hunters appear from around the front of the building holding more bags of food. None of them seemed dead. None of them seemed to have any scars or wounds. They all seemed to be throatful rather than throatless.

"So, Charley," Booker said, stepping toward me. "Thought you could outrun the bad guys, huh?"

"Don't you mean bad *guy*?" I said.

"You totally underestimate us," he said as Fitz and Staley approached. "You honestly thought that *us*, the real Monster Squad, would fall to a *single* demonic entity?"

Fitz and Staley laughed. Barton and Stek continued to talk a few paces away. I noticed that their discussion had fallen into hushed tones, but I overheard Barton reassuring Stek that "she" couldn't possibly show up "there." Whatever that meant.

"Well," I responded, "I *did* see you guys fall to a 'single demonic entity.' I saw *you in particular* get your fucking throat ripped out."

Booker's eyes bulged. He reached up with both hands and grabbed his neck, making a choking sound. Then he stopped, relaxed, and pointed directly at me. "You got a thing or two to learn about *teamwork*, mon friar."

Thankfully, Steve decided to intercede on my behalf. "And *you* got a thing or two to learn about French, dude. Let's drop the macho bullshit and get on with stuff."

Booker laughed and stepped back over to Barton and Stek. Fitz and Staley had gotten back in the car to eat. Screeching guitar music began to emanate from within; it sounded like old-school Megadeth.

I nodded my head in the direction of the hunters and spread my hands.

Steve took the cue. "After I jumped through that portal, I got kicked out down a ways from here," Steve said. He took another drag off of his cigarette. "I tried to hitch a ride back, but it was the middle of the fucking night. I saw these guys on the shoulder of the road, and I was like, 'Hey, aren't you guys those monster hunters?' And we all decided to get some dinner."

"You came through the portal between two stone gateposts?" I asked.

"Yeah," Steve said. "How did you know?"

"Long story," I said. "I'll tell you sometime. Meanwhile, I think Stek's got a plan."

"Is it a good one?" Steve asked.

"Probably not," I said. "Ever been to Tulsa?"

"JUST TRY AND DANCE *around* them!"

This from Booker, who had apparently been shot at numerous times.

I ran for my life, hoping that swift enough movement in near-darkness (and the presence of additional targets) might just save my life. I could see Max Plunkett's shed off in the distance.

More gunshots rang out, this time accompanied by wild redneck hollering. This latter sound terrified me even more than death by bullet—what would that crazed maniac do to those merely *crippled* by a gunshot wound?

Steve had already made it to the shed. He waved at me from the darkened doorway.

I thought I heard two of the other hunters possibly firing *back* at Max Plunkett as I dove into the darkness of the shed. Stek followed, then Booker. Miraculously, amidst more hooting and shots exchanged, the remaining three hunters made it into the shed.

All the firing and noise from outside stopped.

"He won't fire at his shed," Stek said. "Something about those rednecks and their property."

I was still trying to catch my breath in the stuffy, gasoline-scented confines as three of the hunters made their way to the large door leading to the cellar in back. Fitz was barring the front door.

"At least now we know," Steve said, still breathing heavily, "that Chris Baxter was *not* full of shit."

I nodded. Steve helped me up. We followed the hunters, who had unlatched the door and headed down.

The cellar below was just as empty and clean as in the video we had seen of it. And there, shimmering darkly in the middle of the room, stood the portal.

"You guys do this regularly?" Steve asked.

Staley nodded. "Family tradition, now," he said, chuckling. Fitz came down the steps after us. The other hunters were checking their gear. Steve and I had both managed to hang onto our backpacks; I hoped that the key would still prove to be of some use in Tulsa.

Stek turned to the hunters. "Ready when you are," he said. He looked over at me and Steve. We nodded.

One by one, beginning with Fitz, the hunters stepped through the portal, followed by Stek.

"After you," Steve said, gesturing toward the darkness. "I mean, since I fucked up the last time. Your turn."

MORE GUNSHOTS, ALMOST IMMEDIATELY. Steve and I both collapsed to the floor.

"Check him." That was Booker's voice. I peered up in terror as Staley turned on a massive flashlight.

"Steve?" I whispered.

"You guys can get up," Booker said. I pushed myself up off the floor. Several flashlight beams illuminated the room from the video. I found myself lying on an intricate design painted in black on the concrete floor. Staley had focused his flashlight on a prostrate body. Stek.

"What the *fuck* have you guys done?" I shouted. Steve had backed up nearer to the portal again, probably assuming we would need to make a rapid escape. I appreciated the fact that he didn't just leap through and leave me to deal with this.

"Calm down, dude," Booker said. Fitz was riffling through Stek's clothes. He removed his backpack. "The guy was dirty."

"Dirty?" I said.

"Yes, *dirty*," Booker repeated. "As in unclean, bad, double-crossing. Good riddance."

I made a move toward Stek, but Barton halted my passage with a firm arm and a handgun.

"Let him go," Booker said. I didn't bother moving any closer to Stek even after Barton removed his hand from my arm. What good would it do now?

"Got it," Fitz said. He withdrew the wrapped flask of Witch's Wine from Stek's backpack.

"Oh, *shit*," I said. "*That's* what you guys were after? Why didn't you just take it from him in Golem Creek?"

"Didn't know if we could get it through that portal on our own," Booker said. "Experience, kid. Get some."

Fitz placed the flask carefully in a steel box in his own backpack. Barton was shifting a large, heavy-looking panel of wood from one wall to reveal an exit into the next room. Staley and Booker were wasting no time rolling Stek's body into a large canvas tarp.

"I can't fucking believe this," I said. I turned to Steve. He raised his eyebrows at me and jerked a thumb toward the portal.

"Go for it," Booker said, handing Staley a roll of duct tape. "You guys are cool. You want to go back? We're not stopping you."

"I'm not going *anywhere* until I get an explanation!" I said. "You're claiming that Stek double-crossed someone? Well, great, fine, okay. But he was supposed to help us find Julie!"

"He wasn't going to help you find *shit*, man," Booker responded. Staley and Fitz were hefting the body through the hole in the wall. "He worked for Curwen Flowers. His whole plan was to get Mike Flowers back into Laban's tomb and then open that fucking hellhole."

I was stunned. "Why would he *do* that?" I asked.

"Because Curwen promised him all the usual, dude," Booker responded. "Money, power, blah, blah, blah. The dude *fell* for it. But Curwen knew he would. That whole family, man. Bunch of fucking manipulators."

I recalled my own "revelation" concerning Mike's long-term plan involving me, Julie, and Steve. My heart began to sink at thoughts of Julie. Where the hell was she?

The hunters had all gone through the hole in the wall. "You guys coming, or what?" Barton asked. "'Cause I'm gonna close this one way or the other."

I looked over at Steve. There was nothing we could do by going *back*—that seemed almost certain. Whatever "plan" Stek had had, it involved the Witch's Wine. Steve gave me a quick look, then headed for the hole in pursuit of the hunters. I followed.

"WE'RE GOING TO NEED that key, Chuck," Booker said.

Steve and I sat in the back of a large, black van in the parking lot of the McFarlin Library at the University of Tulsa.

I opened my backpack and extracted the key, which glinted softly by the parking lot lights. The van had been stationed out behind CJ's Bar, along with a dark-colored station wagon of unidentifiable make. Barton and Staley had taken the station wagon, loaded with the body, presumably to some predetermined "dump site."

The notion gave me chills. Our semi-captors had then wasted no time in heading for the university. In response to my questions, and a few comments from the clearly perturbed Steve Chernowski, we gleaned that the hunters were probably right about Stek.

"The guy knew about the *vinum sabbati*, after all," Booker said. "How did he get *that* information? This stuff needs to go right back where it belongs, man: buried along with Laban in the Murk."

"I'm still pretty unclear about one thing," I said. "I *know* that I saw you guys get torn apart out there. You're acting like somehow I didn't see what I *know* I saw—"

"All right, sorry," Booker said. "It's true. I haven't explained one piece of the puzzle. But that's because we're sworn to secrecy about it. I'll just be straight with you. If this all works out, I'm sure it will come clear in the end."

I resigned myself to this explanation.

"Well, thanks a lot, dude," Steve finally said. He had been silent for so long I thought perhaps he had been shot in the portal cellar, and hidden it as he gradually bled out in the van. "I mean, that will help us with motivation, and all that shit."

Booker sighed. "Look, I'm sorry, all right? But seriously. If I say a *word* about how we survived that attack, *my* mission is shot. Right in the nuts."

Steve chuckled. "That was good, man," he said. "'Right in the nuts.' I'm gonna *remember* that one."

It got me laughing, too. And when Fitz joined in, I suddenly felt like maybe we might at least survive the night. If not the morning after.

BOOKER HAD A PASSKEY that got us into the McFarlin Library after hours. We took a side door. A small huddle of giggling Asian students were in a crowd at the end of the hall, but they paid absolutely no attention to us as we passed.

Booker led us through a pair of heavy metal doors into a lobby with a checkout counter in the center and a mini café behind it. A wide set of stairs led down to our left, but Booker headed to the far side of the room and a smaller set of stairs beside a pair of elevators, these leading up.

"I thought we looked pretty conspicuous," I said to Steve as we followed the two hunters up the stairs. "You think those kids are going to call security?"

Steve shrugged. "This is a college campus. I'm guessing we look as conspicuous as any other college student," he answered. "Plus, if they *do*, I have a feeling Booker and Co. will have no issue making short work of them."

"True enough," I said. We went up five flights of stairs, Booker and Fitz seeming to practically *slide* up them while Steve and I kept up with a degree of discomfort.

We finally reached our destination, exiting into the middle of a hallway. To our right was a door labeled "Special Collections"; Booker headed left and slowed his pace to a crawl near an unassuming door just before the hall exit. He tapped on it in a weird, rhythmic fashion, and it opened.

Barton cracked the door open. "Good," Booker said. "Let's move."

Barton and Staley exited the room.

"How did they get here so fast?" I asked Steve, who shook his head.

"My question," Steve said, "is where did they dump the body?"

We all assembled before the very small door of what appeared to be a very small, very old elevator.

"The key," Booker said, holding out his hand to me. I flipped open my backpack and pulled it out. It appeared to be emitting a silvery radiance when I handed it to him.

"This is going to be a tight fit," he said as he

hit the elevator button, and when the door opened, I saw why.

"Can we even fit *three* people in there?" Steve asked.

Booker shrugged. "Another goddamned failsafe, man. Laban didn't want any armies getting to the other side."

I shook my head. "But this is *ridiculous*," I said. Fitz, Staley, and Barton had already squeezed into the tiny compartment. There seemed to be about enough room for one, maybe two more very thin people, but after some adjustment, Booker was able to press himself in against the rest of us.

The elevator lurched uncomfortably as the door closed.

"I don't think this thing was designed to carry much more than a couple hundred pounds," Steve said. "If that much."

Booker pressed his palm against a panel on the wall just above our heads; it opened, revealing a simple lock that was obviously designed for the Silver Key. He inserted the key, and the elevator began to hum noisily. Then he hit the button on the floor direction panel labeled with a little star, and the elevator shuddered into movement.

"Normally, this thing gets you to the reserve stacks for Special Collections," he said. "They've actually got some cool shit. Native American skulls and stuff like that. Barton worked here when he was finishing his first Ph.D." I heard him grunt in affirmation behind me. *First* Ph.D.? Who the fuck *were* these guys? "When we finally did all the surveying, we found out that this is exactly where

Laban's tomb should be. The overlay, I mean."

"Overlay?" I repeated.

"Right," Booker continued. The elevator, struggling to carry us all, was certainly taking its time. "Where Laban's dream overlaps this world. McFarlin-fucking-Tower! It makes perfect sense: the tomb is the pyramid and, in a sense, the pyramid is constructed *right on top* of McFarlin Tower." He paused for a moment as the elevator started slowly screeching to a halt. "Or, they're both occupying the same space. Kind of. You get what I mean?"

The elevator stopped. "All right, kids," Booker said. "Let's party."

The door opened and we stepped out into a cold stone room with high ceilings. On a grand platform about twenty feet to our right was a miniature step pyramid, at the top of which hovered an oval portal that I could immediately sense radiating a *massive* degree of power. There even appeared to be a small breeze blowing out of it into the room.

We all tumbled out into the room. Other than the portal, there was a second level in a sort of ring above us, with metal catwalks lining the walls, which were set with shelves and boxes all around.

Booker handed me back the key. "Thanks," he said. "See? Not a fucking villain."

I gave him a weak half-smile in response. Steve was gazing in awe at the portal. Staley and Barton had taken up positions at the foot of the step pyramid. They appeared to be glancing around the room in a confused fashion.

Had I missed something?

"Okay?" Booker turned to Fitz, who shrugged.

What the hell was going on? "Um. Gimme the stuff," Booker continued, as if stalling. "We don't know for sure what's on the other side of that portal." He began to sound more confident. But was he faking it? "And we sure as *shit* don't want to have to do this *twice*. If we even can."

Fitz had removed his pack and taken out the little steel box with the Witch's Wine in it. As he handed it over to Booker, we heard Staley yell.

"Incoming!" he screamed. Something plummeted from above. I had barely enough time to dive for cover, followed by Steve, as a slew of boxes and junk started avalanching onto us.

I heard clattering, grunting, and struggling but, thankfully, no gunshots rang out. Dust had billowed up around us. One or two of the hunters yelled out a handful of swear words.

Steve and I both looked up at the same time. I discerned a shape, a person, diving into the portal.

"He got the stuff!" Booker screamed. *"After him!"*

"Who?" I yelled.

"Mike Flowers!" Booker yelled, scampering up the steps of the pyramid. *"You motherfu—"*

Another avalanche of boxes came from above. Apparently, Mike had set up a trip wire or something on the steps of the pyramid. Steve and I only missed the brunt of the cascading rubble by hanging back behind the action. I heard more groans.

I looked at Steve. There was only one thing we could do, one possible course of action with the Monster Squad down for the count and time not waiting for any man. We both leapt up at the same time and charged the portal.

"*Right in the nuts!*" I heard Steve yell as we both launched ourselves through the blackness, into a different blackness.

WE LANDED, RATHER PAINFULLY, on granite.

Steve was groaning a few feet away. I rolled over on my back and checked for broken bones. I couldn't discern any, although I was bloody enough from skinning my arms on rock from the awkward fall.

"Steve!" I said, coming to my senses. I glanced around. Another large stone room, a high arched ceiling, maybe twenty or thirty feet up, stone walls, weird tapestries with heraldic emblems on them, torchlight glinting off stones—

"Charles Leland." The voice came from just behind me. I turned my head. "And Stephanos Chernowski."

Standing before a large rectangular stone sarcophagus at the center of the room, gazing down at me and Steve with his usual perfect calm, was Michael Flowers.

"My students," he said. "What have you learned during my unintended absence?"

"That you're a thieving *sonofabitch*," said Steve, standing up.

I winced, but no lightning bolts followed, no death curses or tortuous words of power blasted us. In fact, as I looked intently at Michael Flowers, I noticed that he seemed to be struggling with something. He looked, perhaps, as if he was *grieving*.

"And you, Charles?" Mike asked.

I hesitated. Why did he look so *sad* to me all of a sudden?

"Tell him, Charley!" Steve shouted. "Tell him he's a conniving fucker! I'll back you up. He can't kill the both of us—at least, not quickly—"

"Nothing," I answered Mike. Steve shut up. "I've learned—*absolutely*—*fucking*—*nothing*!" I noticed that I was trembling.

"Go on," Mike responded.

"No!" I yelled. I staggered toward him. "No! I don't want to. I want to go *home*. I want Julie back. I'm tired of this *bullshit*." I waved my hand around the room.

Mike pulled out a dagger as I approached him. "Go ahead!" I screamed at him. "Go ahead! Cut my throat. Whatever. I'm not going to stop you. I'm just looking for the exit!"

"I wish you would," he said.

"Find the *exit*?" Steve said behind me.

"Stop me," Mike corrected him. He held the dagger out to me, hilt first. "Because otherwise—" he hesitated for a moment. "Otherwise. I'll have to try to do it myself again."

"Jesus, Mike," Steve said. "What *is* this—"

"All about *peace*," Mike said, lowering the dagger and turning to face the sarcophagus. "It was all about finding some peace. That was what Laban wanted. He saw what was to come."

"Yeah, well, he sure chose one hell of a way to solve that problem," I said. "What did he expect? *Those creatures are going to get out*, Mike! The Murk—*every* 'Murk,' every crack in the worlds—they're all going to overflow. And those guys you just knocked out back there, they're trying to *stop* it—"

"No, they're not," Mike said. "They're Molly's slaves. She saw the opportunity when Wryneck slaughtered them—"

"Wryneck?" Steve said.

"The creature from the Murk. The one that Pete Jarry learned to partially control—and infected with his strange tastes in the process of bonding with him," Mike explained. "Those men out there had one purpose for you. Without the keyholder, they could never access this place. Once they had made their way here, once they had opened the gates for those creatures from the pit to flood this world, they would have made short work of you—if they had even needed to, at that point. You saw what happened to Stek after they'd gotten what they needed from him."

Steve made an exasperated noise. "My mind is officially blowing," he said, "like, right this fucking second."

I suddenly made the connection. "They *were* stalling, out there," I said. "They were waiting—for *Molly*. She was supposed to be here—"

"A knotty issue I took some trouble to disentangle," Mike said. "Although the threads of it have yet to be re-woven, in light of our present emergency."

As if to punctuate this utterance, a deep and abysmal rumbling emanated from within the stone casket.

"Mike," I spoke carefully, "we have *no way* of knowing if what you're saying is true. You hand me that dagger, and I 'kill' you—if you even *can* be killed—what does that accomplish? Why not just let those guys out *there* kill you? Why us? Why *me*?"

"Curwen's blood," he said. "In that timestream where you made a pact with the Fairy Queen, you communicated your *blood* to her. This damned Molly to be the Witch's plaything until she stole her body and took her place. A curse and a blessing. You became a part of the pact—a part of Curwen's *bloodline*—yet another way into and out of the Murk."

"But *I* didn't do that—" I insisted.

"That doesn't matter!" Mike said. "It doesn't matter at all. We are an infinity of selves, all living out all possible lives, *but there is that which remains.* A spark—something 'you' throughout all of it—that suffers the curses of the lot. And the occasional blessing, perhaps, when some iota of intelligence seeps out of one's *idios kosmos*—"

"I know what that *means!*" Steve exclaimed, clapping his hands.

"Where do you think the Oriental traditions got the notion of karma, anyway?" Mike finished, oblivious to Steve's outburst. "Something owed; cause and effect. But the magicians found a means of escape—and it was Laban's attempt to *make* a heaven for himself, a place where his dreams would remain safe and timeless, in lieu of any other heaven, the likes of which he could not locate no matter how far he traveled in any realm."

Mike leaned against the stone. I could see over the edge now, into a deep blackness. He seemed tired.

"Final lesson," he said. "And now I need your help. We must invalidate Curwen's scheme. Laban *cannot return*. Please accept my apologies for the extent to which vested interests have taken this simple plan. I really thought—perhaps, years ago—that it may not need to come to this."

He lifted the dagger to me again. "It must be you," he said. "When I sprinkle the *vinum sabbati* into this grave, when I speak the final banishing, you will plunge the dagger into my heart. *His blood only can destroy me.* And you will ensure that I am fallen into this blackness. It is our only chance to seal the gate. It is our only chance to preserve Laban's dreaming, if not the remainder of the world."

"'If not the remainder'?" Steve said. "I thought Laban was like the cork in the bottle? If the gate gets sealed, why would the world still get flooded?"

"It was never our decision to make," Mike said. "We could only create the Place of Solace, and hope that the various places of overlap would be tended to by those with the knowledge to do so."

"Seems kind of anticlimactic," Steve said.

Mike grinned at him. "Let the Lords of Chaos be the judge of that," he said. "Who knows what miracles lie at the farther edge of infinity?"

I took the dagger from him.

"You can't be *serious*, Charley?" Steve said. "Don't—I mean, maybe we can figure something else out—"

Coughing and sputtering, someone slammed onto the granite floor from the portal.

"Quickly, now!" Mike said. He began muttering

to himself as he uncapped the flask of Witch's Wine. "You must do it *right as I complete the utterances!*"

"*Son of a bitch! Where is she?*" It was Booker's voice, screaming. Two more bodies were suddenly in the room. "Get that stuff before he empties it!"

Steve slammed into one of them. My heart was thumping through my chest. Mike had entered some kind of trance, and continued to mutter as he dribbled the contents of the flask into Laban's grave. A shimmering iridescence began to emanate out of the blackness within, and a purplish-mauve mist began seeping out over the edges of the stone walls.

I heard more scuffling. I lifted the dagger and prayed mentally for *just enough time—*

"Get off of me!" That was Booker's voice. "Barton! Get him! *Do something!*"

A peculiar bright-pink glow began emanating from *me. Why was I glowing?*

I looked down. The source of illumination appeared to be my *left pants pocket.* I reached within it—and clasped my fingers around the little plastic sandwich sword. I pulled it out of my pocket and held it out in front of me, on my open palm.

The lunch ornament began to grow, both in weight and in size, remaining a translucent, glimmering, radiant pink nonetheless. Inadvertently, I dropped it, and it clattered onto the stone floor.

I chanced a look behind me, and almost dropped the dagger in amazement. It *was* Steve—but it *wasn't*—it was—

"Graxx!" I shouted. Steve/Graxx the Half-Elf Thief was holding his own against three of the hunters, who crowded into the room.

But where was—

Booker lunged around the opposite side of the portal. He shrieked, a looked of crazed fury twisting his face, as he sprinted for Mike, then leapt for the flask of Witch's Wine, hands outstretched, fearing neither fate nor anything.

Of its own volition, the sword—now full-size—lifted itself vertically, point upward, and levitated to a spot directly over the shimmering blackness of Laban's grave. Immediately, there was silence, utter and complete. Booker and the other hunters froze—both in *time* as well as in *space*—spellbound, their eyes transfixed by the radiant Hot-Pink Sandwich Sword That Could.

Steve's/Graxx's eyes widened. "The Sword of Astonishment!" he yelled. "That's *it*!"

"What do I—" I started.

Before I could finish speaking, Mike leapt onto the edge of the stone wall of Laban's grave, then directly onto the point of the glimmering, hovering sword. A look of bewilderment crossed his features. Blood burst forth from the wounds in his chest and back.

"I'm—" he said. Weakly, he lifted his face in an attempt to regard me. The sword held fast, still floating above the pool of shimmering color now mixing with his heart's blood. Something like a smile crept into the grimace of pain on his face. He wavered uncertainly, blinking a stream of tears out of his eyes, coughing blood. "*I'm—sorry.* I—never meant—"

He collapsed utterly, along with the sword, into

the cavernous tomb. One last burst of radiant color, shimmering, blindingly bright, cascaded out and around the stone room.

I fell back against the ground.

When I opened my eyes, the room appeared roughly as it had been when we entered it. Steve stood where the portal once was, gazing at the little figure of Graxx in the palm of his hand.

"The Silent Goblin Gang," Steve said, shaking his head and smiling. "I should have fucking known." He looked up at me and waved his hand at the four bodies collapsed around the room—now four piles of dust, merely remains of the corpses they had always been.

THE PORTAL BACK TO Tulsa had disintegrated the moment Michael Flowers sealed the gate in Laban's tomb. Steve and I managed to find an exit behind one of the tapestries in the room.

"The right-hand portal!" Steve said as we exited into the room at the base of the stairs leading out. "God*damn* my luck!"

Our trek back out and down the pyramid was colored with a weirdly increasing sense of elation. Steve couldn't be brought down; he constantly made D & D references, and replayed the scene of his battle with the "Silent Goblin Gang" at least four times. I noticed the play-by-play getting increasingly elaborate with each repetition.

"Were you *really* gonna stab him, though?" he asked me as we stood in the fresh air of the Place of Solace, gazing out in the direction of the Dream-keeper's Emporium. "I mean, seriously? Really?"

"I don't know," I said. I wrapped up the Silver Key, shoved it into my backpack, and pulled out a dented can of—

"Milwaukee's Best?" Steve shrugged. I cracked it open and let the watery sludge fizzle out for a moment onto the side of the pyramid. "I guess so."

Steve pulled out his flask and took a swig. "This is the best-tasting liquor in the entire universe," he said, and took another.

I guzzled the awful beer and tossed the can aside. "I think I'm going to need several handfuls of painkillers," I said, gingerly peeling back one of my shirt sleeves.

Steve handed me an orange pill bottle without hesitation. "I already took one on our way up."

"Do you think Julie's—" I started.

"—at the Emporium?" Steve finished. "God, I hope so. I mean, who the fuck else are we going to tell the end of this story to? Roland? Something tells me he already knows it."

As we strolled through the empty streets, marveling at the place and its infinite beauty, I formed a plan. I had a sinking feeling that Julie *wasn't* going to be there when we arrived.

But I had another feeling, a better one, that Julie was alive and well, and like the way the rooms in the Dreamkeeper's Emporium would seem to change to accommodate what you expected and desired, if I could remember all of our story, every last detail, then we would find her again, and we could all come back here together to this wonderful, safe, and happy place.

epilogue

THE

GODS

ARE

FORGETFUL

YES! THE GODS ARE forgetful. But we humans can be even *more* so—and with less good reason.

That is why Julie Evergreen did everything in her power to preserve the memory of what had happened in that flotsam of mind-stuff she knew as Golem Creek. It was a *real place*; this formed the basic premise of her existential argument. Whether it was *idios kosmos* or *koinos kosmos*—that remained to be seen. But it was *real*.

This she knew; this she kept to herself.

There had been a blip, a deletion, a skip in the record. That was the portal, the shimmering darkness in Laban Black's tomb.

Then awakening to her alarm clock. But it was— Fall Break. First semester at the university. She was going to have to drive back home tomorrow for Thanksgiving at her parents' house in Oklahoma City.

This also she remembered.

But she would need *something* to read—something *not school related*—to get through *that* trip.

So that's what she would do. She'd head to Gardner's today and get a couple of used books. Enjoy herself tonight. Drive out some time tomorrow, make it to OKC by evening.

GARDNER'S BOOKS WAS THE usual chaos of stuff piled everywhere, but at least it was kind of quiet today.

Julie headed over to the fantasy paperbacks. As usual, she couldn't see much on the top-top shelf, nor on the bottom-bottom shelf, without a bit of straining. Damned aisles barely large enough for *her*, and she fell easily below the featherweight range. What about all those massive Tulsans out there? The ones who seemed to make a regular habit of restaurant-hopping?

She ran her fingers over some of the titles. So many old friends here...she skipped through the names, desperate for something she hadn't already read. *Bellairs...de Camp...Duane...Heinlein...Herbert...Lackey...Le Guin...Leland...*

Her hand stopped instinctively.

Leland.

A battered paperback. She could barely make out the title from the spine. She pulled it out from the shelf, and her breath caught.

Fear Club: A Confession, she read. By Charles T. Leland.

The cover was a panorama, marred by numerous white creases, bends, folds, and tears. The image on the front had been mercilessly battered, but she could *almost* make out the likenesses of three figures. They were in a cemetery, it seemed, hovering around a grave.

The first few pages appeared to have been torn or fallen out, but a super-weird "dedication" page before the start of the book proper remained.

Box 1132
(I'm pretty sure it will work.)

Julie noticed a rush of blood to her head, her heart pounding, as she started to turn the dedication page.

Someone bumped into her from the side.

"Oh! Pardon me!" a girl's voice said as Julie turned around. "Cramped aisles."

The scent of strawberry licorice and bubble gum met Julie's nostrils in force mere moments before sight of the girl's unparalleled magnificence. Julie stepped back inadvertently, unready for the potent onslaught.

"It's—fine, really," Julie said. How did one choose words in the presence of such a creature? "I was just—"

"Interesting book," the girl said, gazing at *Fear Club*.

"Have you read this?" Julie asked, waving a copy of the book before her. Gods, the girl was beautiful...but the uncanny aura about her seemed even to absorb any sensations of littleness or lack Julie might otherwise have felt outside of its radiance.

"Oh, that one?" she answered. "Yes, I have."

Julie felt herself practically trembling with excitement.

"So you think I should—" she began.

"You should," the girl said. She put one immaculately manicured hand on Julie's shoulder and gazed directly in her eyes. Pools of fire—that's what Julie thought she saw in them. Pools of lavender-tinged fire. "In fact, I *insist* that you read it. And let me know what you think?"

The girl removed her hand from Julie's shoulder and extracted the book from the latter's benumbed grip. Moments later she handed it back, having inscribed her name and phone number on the inside front cover.

"Give me a call once you finish it," she said. "Any time."

"Any time?" Julie repeated in a daze. "You'll answer?"

"Yes," Molly replied. "I will. Yes."

THE END of BOOK ONE

Former head of the now-defunct "Werewolf Coven" (1987-1995) and occasional college mathematics instructor **DAMIAN STEPHENS** lives at the edge of a dark forest in Virginia, within which he can often be found chanting baleful incantations to Yog Sothoth or evoking demons from the Pit to physical appearance. Currently, his research includes: applications of Bruno's *De umbris idearum* to quantum entanglement (via microtubule configuration); fractal multiplication of the *elixir rubeus* (macroscopic treatment); Vaihinger's *Die Philosophie des Als Ob* as Husserlian device in many-worlds travel; "PDEs and Parzival: The Differential Geometry of Mithridatist [sic] Architecture" (a presentation for the Noisy Bridge Rod & Gun Club) ; and an encyclopedic analysis of agonistic tropes in *Finnegans Wake*. All of these themes and more are pursued, heavily camouflaged, in his fiction. Send him an email care of

info@fourthmansions.com